íVERS!

The Pirate Who's Afraid of EVERYTHING

BY **ANNABETH BONDOR-STONE**
AND **CONNOR WHITE**

ILLUSTRATED BY **ANTHONY HOLDEN**

BASED ON A REALLY FUNNY IDEA BY
HARRISON BLANZ, AGE 9

HARPER
An Imprint of HarperCollinsPublishers

Shivers!: The Pirate Who's Afraid of Everything
Text copyright © 2015 by Annabeth Bondor-Stone and Connor White
Illustrations copyright © 2015 by Anthony Holden

Library of Congress Cataloging-in-Publication Data
Bondor-Stone, Annabeth.
  Shivers: the pirate who's afraid of everything / by Annabeth Bondor-Stone and Connor
White ; based on a really funny idea by Harrison Blanz ; illustrated by Anthony Holden. –
First edition.
    pages cm
  ISBN 978-0-06-231387-4 (hardback)
  [1. Pirates–Fiction. 2. Fear–Fiction. 3. Adventure and adventurers–Fiction.
4. Humorous stories.] I. White, Connor. II. Holden, Anthony, illustrator. III. Title. IV. Title:
Pirate who is afraid of everything.
PZ7.1.B665Pir 2015   2014022684
[Fic]–dc23   CIP
                                                                                                       AC

Typography by Joe Merkel
15 16 17 18 19 PC/RRDH 10 9 8 7 6 5 4 3 2 1
❖
First Edition

BEEP-BEEP

BEEP-BEEP

BEEP-BEEP

BEEP-

CHAPTER ONE

"BEEP-BEEP! BEEP-BEEP!"

Shivers the Pirate sat up in bed and screamed, "AGHH! BREACH OF PERIMETER!"

He bolted out of bed and looked frantically around his sleeping quarters. He knew that the beeping sound meant there was some kind of danger on his pirate ship.

"BEEP-BEEP! BEEP-BEEP!" The noise continued.

Shivers stumbled down the ship's passageway as fast as he could, wailing, "LOCK THE DOORS! LOAD THE CANNONS! SWAB THE POOP DECK!"

Shivers knew it was time to start his Emergency Attack Plan.

First, he threw on his helmet.

Then, he reinforced the walls of his fort.

Finally, he grabbed his trusted first mate, Albee.

He leaped into the fort and called out, "Show yourself, you yellow-bellied son of a cow's liver!"

But no one responded.

The only sound was that constant "BEEP-BEEP! BEEP-BEEP!"

Shivers turned to Albee and said, "Perhaps we're not under attack . . . perhaps it's

. . . THE GREAT STORM!"

Shivers jumped out of his fort and ran around in circles, shouting, "TRIM THE SAIL! BATTEN DOWN THE HATCHES! SWAB THE POOP DECK!"

Then he ran to the porthole to see the destruction from the massive hurricane!

But the sky was sunny and blue. There wasn't a single cloud in sight.

The noise wouldn't stop. "BEEP-BEEP! BEEP-BEEP!"

With fear in his eyes, Shivers yelled out the window, "IT'S AN ALIEN ATTACK! IT'S THE END OF THE WORLD! IT'S–"

Shivers cowered in the corner next to his bed and realized what was really making the sound.

"–MY ALARM CLOCK!" he shouted.

In one brave motion, Shivers raised his arm and smashed the snooze button! The beeping stopped. Shivers breathed a sigh of relief.

"Well, that's about enough adventure for one day," he said. "I just wish this didn't happen *every* morning."

Now it was time for Shivers to shut down his Emergency Attack Plan. He took off his helmet, which was really just a big soup bowl. He tore down the fort, which was really just a bunch of pillows wrapped in a blanket.

He gave Albee a handful of fish flakes. Albee, you see, is a fish. And Shivers's best friend.

Shivers was about to go brush his teeth, when suddenly his stomach felt like he had just eaten a bowlful of caterpillars. "I'm afraid I'm getting seasick," he moaned in Albee's general direction.

But really, it was impossible for Shivers to be seasick. Like all pirates, Shivers lived on a ship. However, unlike all pirates, his ship had never been to sea. It was docked on the sand at New Jersey Beach. Shivers's pirate ship had never been to sea because Shivers was completely terrified of the sea. In fact, Shivers was terrified of everything that had to do with being a pirate. It was a *real* problem.

💀 💀 💀

Shivers came from a family of famous pirates. His mom was known as "Tilda the Tormentor!" because she once tied up and taunted an entire army of vicious sea creatures without coming up for air! His dad was known as "Bob!" because his name was Bob. But Bob was also an awesome pirate!

mom

Brock

Dad

Shivers

Shivers had a brave older brother named Brock. Brock loved being a pirate and wasn't afraid of anything. Brock and Shivers had nothing in common. When Shivers was born, his parents named him after the famous pirate saying "Shiver Me Timbers!" Now Shivers was eleven years old, and his name ended up being perfect because he spent most of his time afraid of one thing or another, shaking and shivering in a corner.

☠ ☠ ☠

And this morning had been no different. As Shivers looked out his bedroom porthole to the beach, he hoped to see his parents' pirate ship the *Plunderer* bobbing on the waves. Whenever his parents returned from a pirate mission, the first thing they always did was drop anchor on the shore and walk across the beach to pay Shivers a visit, scaring away all the sunbathers in their path. Then they would tell Shivers stories of their pirate adventures.

Shivers squinted into the sun, looking as far as he could but the *Plunderer* was nowhere in sight. He thought his family should be back by now. "I guess adventures sometimes take longer than expected," he said. He shrugged and decided to start his day. He put on his bunny slippers and padded into the kitchen, carrying Albee with him in his fishbowl. "My mom always says breakfast is the best way to start the day."

Albee waved his fins in agreement.

Shivers put a big bag of popcorn in the microwave and covered his ears until the popping was over. Then he put the popcorn in a bowl and began the day's work.

He and Albee were in the midst of an epic and dangerous quest to trap and safely remove a ladybug that had crawled into Shivers's boot last week. As you can imagine, the quest ended with Shivers cowering in the corner.

Today he decided to try again by lowering a leaf into the boot to scoop out the little bug. But just as he finished putting on his safety gloves, a pigeon

landed on the windowsill
with a flutter. Shivers whirled
around and let out a sound that was
halfway between a squeak and a burp.

"Don't come any closer, pigeon!" he warned.
But pigeons are not good listeners. The pigeon
spread her wings again and took flight, knock-
ing Shivers's daisy plant off the windowsill and
smashing it onto the ground. She flew in circles
around the kitchen, crashing into plates, shatter-
ing glasses, and spilling popcorn everywhere.

At last, the pigeon landed on top of the refrigera-
tor, and Shivers breathed a sigh of relief. "That was
close. I thought she was flying right at my"–Shivers
screamed–"HEAD!" as the pigeon took off again
and flew right at his head, cooing and flapping like
crazy. Shivers raised his hands. "I surrender! You
can have all the popcorn you want!" At the last
second, the pigeon veered away from Shivers and
landed on the table. She stuck out her foot and
Shivers noticed that there was a letter tied to it.

"Oh, you're a carrier pigeon!" Shivers sighed. "I have to stop thinking that every pigeon is just out to steal my popcorn."

Shivers untied the string, opened the letter, and began to read:

To our dear son Shivers—

Shivers jumped up with glee. "It's a letter from my mom and dad! I can't wait to hear how much treasure they've plundered!"

He continued reading.

We miss you so much! Have you had breakfast today? We hope you're doing well. We're doing TERRIBLY! We were on a pirate mission on the Eastern Seas. All was going well until we were captured on a distant island. This place is like nothing you've ever seen, Shivers. It's overrun by dogs! There are fairies everywhere! And they all worship a great green giant!

Shivers turned to Albee and said, "This is terrible! I'd better call my brave brother, Brock. He'll be able to save them! I'll do that as soon as I finish reading."

Shivers read on.

Just so you know, we already called your brave brother, Brock. He came and tried to save us, but now he's captured, too. You're our last hope, Shivers. And now here are detailed directions for how to get to the island. Boy, do I hope the carrier pigeon doesn't poop on this part. First, find the Carnival. When you get there, go to the Fun Hopper and get the map of—

The rest was covered in pigeon poop.

"Oh, gross!" said Shivers. He scowled at the pigeon. "Thanks a lot, pigeon! You ruined the note. You had the entire ocean to poop in and you chose to poop on this letter–WAIT!"

Shivers's eyes nearly popped out of his head as he realized what the letter meant. "My family has been captured, and I'm the last hope they have in the whole world!"

Shivers knew that he had to do something to save his parents. He put on his long velvet coat and his feathered pirate hat. He stepped into his pantaloons, which are big, billowy pants that most pirates use to store treasure but Shivers uses to store popcorn. He would have put on his pirate boots, but the ladybug was still in there, so he stayed in his bunny slippers. They were more comfortable anyway.

He put Albee in a ziplock bag full of water (a fish's favorite way to travel). He fed him a three-course meal of one tiny fish flake, another tiny fish flake, and . . . one last tiny fish flake.

They were ready to go.

He took a deep breath and walked out the front door.

☠ ☠ ☠

As he took his first step off the ship, a massive tidal wave crashed down on his head!

"AGGHH! I'm drowning!" screamed Shivers. "Help! I can't swim!"

He flailed his scrawny arms in the air, trying to stay afloat, until he realized aloud, "Oh. It's just rain."

He grabbed his umbrella and set off on his terrifying journey. He knew he was beginning an epic adventure. He would have to brave the elements and face the dark, scary unknown.

He would have to walk the entire four blocks
to the police station and see if Police Chief
Clomps'n'Stomps would go find his parents
for him.

END OF CHAPTER ONE.

OR IS IT?!?

 →(It is.)

CHAPTER TWO

"FREEZE! PUT YOUR PAWS above your head and back away from the nest!" Margo shouted, flashing her police badge. She was yelling at a raccoon who was getting dangerously close to a nest of bird eggs. Margo was only ten years old, so she wasn't very scary looking. She wasn't even very tall. But she knew she could take care of a raccoon that was up to no good.

"Those little eggs are about to hatch, raccoon!" she yelled. "You stay out of here, or we're taking you downtown!" She stomped her foot and the raccoon scampered away.

"Very good, Margo," said Police Chief Clomps'n'Stomps.

"Thanks, Dad," replied Margo. She slipped her big green backpack off her shoulder and put her police badge in the front pocket. Margo never went anywhere without her big green backpack. It matched her big green eyes. She never went anywhere without those, either.

"I was afraid that raccoon was going to eat those baby birds," Police Chief Clomps'n'Stomps said, beaming proudly.

"Not on my watch!" Margo announced.

Margo and her dad continued on their walk to the police station. Margo loved going to work with her dad. That's why she had convinced him that today was Take Your Daughter to Work Day, even though it was just a regular Tuesday.

Really, she should have been in Mrs. Beezle's fifth-grade class, but she never learned anything useful there. For instance, she knew that today the class would be learning the state capitals and how to do multiplication. Margo already knew the state capitals—and she had a calculator. Margo thought to herself, *Even if Mrs. Beezle is going to let the class play kickball all day long, I would still rather go to the police station with my dad.* There was nothing she loved more in the whole world. Except for maybe . . .

"A pirate!" Margo shouted. "Look, Dad, it's Shivers the Pirate!" She pointed at Shivers, who was pounding on the door of the police station.

Even though Margo had never met Shivers, she knew right away that this boy had to be him. He was wearing pantaloons, so he had to be a pirate. And he was wearing bunny slippers, so he had to be Shivers.

Police Chief Clomps'n'Stomps sighed at the sight of Shivers. In his opinion, pirates should stay at sea and out of the way. Unfortunately, Shivers was a landlubber and too often needed some extra help. "Shivers, I'm sorry," Clomps'n'Stomps said. "We're too busy today to clear the dust out of your closet."

"I would never ask you to do that!" said Shivers.

"You asked me to do that last Thursday," said the chief.

"Well, the dust looked like poisonous spiders!" Shivers explained. "Besides, that's not what I'm here for."

"What, then?" the chief barked. "You need us to get a snail out of your daisies?"

"I do not joke about snails and you *know* that," Shivers said sternly. On the list of Shivers's biggest fears, snails came in at number two. "This is an emergency."

The chief rolled his eyes as he and Margo pushed past Shivers and went inside. "We told you, Shivers, the water is *supposed* to disappear after you take a bath."

"No, but my family—" Shivers tried to explain.

SLAM!

The door flew shut in Shivers's face. Without a hope in the world, he curled into a ball on the police station porch.

All of a sudden, a bright voice called out, "Avast, matey! ARGGH!"

Shivers turned around to see Margo shaking a twig at him.

"AGGH! Get that deadly spear away from me!" Shivers screamed.

"Only if you tell me where the booty is!" she said, covering one eye with the palm of her hand like an eye patch.

"I don't know what 'booty' means, but I don't like the sound of it," Shivers said.

"Booty be treasure!" Margo said, leaping toward Shivers with her twig. "Shouldn't you know that, Shivers the Pirate? Or be you a wet-bellied son of a flotsam?"

"Me? A wet-bellied son of a flotsam?" Shivers asked. "You're a sour-bellied daughter of a biscuit!"

"How dare you?! I'm no biscuit's daughter!" shouted Margo. "Why, I've tied up kidnappers and locked them up to rot. I've tracked down the world's darkest evildoers, and when I was finished with them, they were evil-undoers. And that was just this weekend."

Shivers stared into Margo's big green eyes. "Really?" he asked.

"Yeah!" said Margo. "I'm Officer Margo. I fight bad guys with my dad." Margo took her badge out of her backpack and handed it to Shivers as proof. Shivers couldn't believe that a real police officer was finally giving him the time of day. Maybe she was the one person who could help him.

He decided to tell her all about his captured family. As he told her, he started to panic, so the story sounded something like this:

"Parents! Brock! Treasure! Green! Fairies! Popcorn!! Pigeon poop!!! HEEEEELP!!!!"

"Wait a second," Margo said. "Your parents and brave brother, Brock, are trapped on a distant island overrun by dogs and fairies where everyone worships a green giant. You heard all this from a pooping pigeon and you need my help?"

Shivers collapsed on the police station steps and breathed a sigh of relief. "Exactly."

"Well, let's go find them!" said Margo, beside herself with excitement. She started to wave her stick above her head like a sword.

"Wait! No," Shivers whimpered. "I'll be too afraid."

"You'll be too afraid?" Margo sighed. "So my dad was right about you. You are scared of everything. I guess we can't go on an adventure after all."

Shivers's face turned red. He didn't have any real friends besides Albee, and he had always wanted a friend who wasn't a fish. Margo definitely wasn't a fish, and maybe she could be his friend. He didn't want to let her down but the thought of going on a quest, even if it meant finding his parents and brave brother, Brock, was truly terrifying.

Shivers stammered, "No, wait. . . . I didn't say, '*I'll be* too afraid . . .'" Thinking fast, he held up Albee in his bag and continued, "I said, '*Albee's* too afraid.' Albee is my fish. And my first mate. He's the one who is afraid of everything."

Margo bent down so that she was nose to nose with Albee. At least she thought it was his nose. But no one knows if fishes have noses. Either way, her face was close to his.

"Don't worry, Albee," Margo said in her kindest, fishiest voice. "It's okay to be afraid."

Albee waved his fins at her.

"Courage is not the absence of fear; it's mastery of fear," she continued. "I read that on a cereal box once."

Albee bravely blinked his fishy eyes and swam in a circle in his plastic bag.

"I think he's ready," said Margo. Before Shivers could think of any more excuses,

chew on this:

Courage is not the absence of fear; it's MASTERY of fear. —unknown

Adobe

100% RDA of very helpful advice

FDA approved

Margo launched into her plan. "First, we'll have to prepare your ship. I'll get the supplies, carry them to the ship, and make sure everything is set up for our quest."

Shivers asked, "What should I do?"

Margo thought for a second. "You? Well, hmm . . . why don't you swab the poop deck?"

"Perfect," he said. "The job I was born to do."

They walked together toward the ship, Shivers carrying Albee in his plastic bag. "Wait!" said Margo, stopping in her tracks. "I'll meet you there. There's something I have to take care of."

"But how will you know how to find my ship?" Shivers asked.

"It's the only one docked in the middle of the beach, isn't it?" she asked.

Shivers nodded. "It's next to the snack shop. You'll see people in line for ice cream."

"How did your ship end up in the middle of the beach, anyway?" Margo asked.

"That's an excellent question!" Shivers said. He began to explain.

💀 💀 💀

As a pirate, Shivers was born at sea and expected to spend his whole life there. But when he turned two, Shivers looked at the ocean and spoke his first word:

"AGGGGHHH!"

When he turned five, he became convinced that the ocean was just a giant bowl of soup about to be slurped up at any moment. And when he turned nine, he started dropping the anchor every time his parents tried to set sail. Bob realized that his son wasn't meant to live a life at sea. And he quickly grew tired of lifting the anchor up. It was really heavy!

So, for Shivers's tenth birthday, Bob built him a boat of his own to keep on land. He would have built him a house, but pirates don't know how to build houses. They sink too fast. Tilda never wanted to be too far from Shivers, so she insisted that he park his boat as close to the ocean as possible.

💀 💀 💀

"So that's why I have my own ship parked next to the snack shop on New Jersey Beach," Shivers explained. "And that's why the New Jersey

Beach–goers are always complaining about having to line up around a pirate ship just to get an ice-cream cone."

When Shivers was done speaking, Margo blinked her big green eyes. She had one last question. "Does your ship have a name?"

"It has the perfect name!" Shivers smiled proudly. "The *Land Lady!*"

Margo laughed. "I'll see you at the *Land Lady!*" she cried, jumping in the air. "First, I have to tell my dad where I'm going."

Shivers nodded and headed down the street, looking for any sign of danger while nibbling on popcorn and pantaloon pocket lint.

Margo knocked on the police station door. Chief Clomps'n'Stomps answered. "Dad," she told him. "It's actually not Take Your Daughter to Work Day. It's Sail the Seven Seas Day."

Clomps'n'Stomps shrugged. "I can't argue with that," he said.

CHAPTER THREE

THERE IS SOMETHING YOU don't know about Shivers: He is terrified of street signs. On his way back to the ship, he refused to look at a single street sign, so he got hopelessly lost and didn't arrive for three hours.

By the time he got home, Margo had transformed the *Land Lady* into a fiercely armed vessel of butt-kicking awesomeness. The first thing he noticed was the flag hanging from the ship's mast. Margo had dyed the flag black and drawn a picture of crossed swords underneath the ship's name.

"Do you like it?" asked Margo.

"It makes me want to dig a hole, hide in it, and never come out again," said Shivers.

"So it's perfect!" said Margo as she led Shivers through the ship's front door. She started the grand tour in the sleeping quarters. "I took all your pillowcases and sewed them into a big sack," she said, pointing to a pillowcase sack so big it covered the entire bed.

"Even the satin ones?" Shivers asked.

"Especially the satin ones," Margo replied. Shivers looked disappointed, but she continued, "You see a bad guy: throw him in the sack. Simple. Understand?"

Shivers nodded.

Margo led him to the kitchen and over to the win- dowsill where he kept his potted plants. All of his daisies were gone. The pots were now filled with creepy-  looking plants with sharp, leathery leaves.

"Over here, I got rid of all your daisies and replaced them with Venus flytraps," Margo explained. "If you see a bad guy and the sack is already full, throw a Venus flytrap at him. Simple. Are you with me?"

Shivers nodded again.

Then he followed Margo down the hall and into the bathroom, where she pointed to the bathtub. With a stern look on her face, she said, "This next part is very important. I threw out all your rubber duckies and replaced them with swords. Which means, we have a lot of swords. Oh, and also? Do *not* take a bath. You see a bad guy? He's got a sword? Grab a sword from the tub and use it. Simple. Got it?"

Shivers didn't nod again because all the nodding was giving him a headache. But he understood! "How do you know so much about capturing bad guys?" Shivers asked. "Did you learn it at school?"

Margo was confused. "Of course not, Shivers. I learned it from my dad. You don't learn those kinds of things at school."

"Pirate kids don't go to school," Shivers explained. "They learn everything they need to know while they're on missions with their parents. It's on-the-job training."

"But you don't go on missions," said Margo. "Don't you get bored?"

"Bored?" Shivers laughed. "Clearly, you've never played a game of Go Fish with Albee."

Margo narrowed her eyes at Albee, who was swimming circles in his bag. "How could you play cards with Albee?"

"Cards? What do you mean?" Shivers asked. "I put him in his bowl and I yell, 'Go, Fish!' and he swims around as fast as he can. We do it for six hours every day, and by then, it's nap time. Then it's song and dance time, and then we call it a day. School wouldn't even fit in my schedule."

Margo nodded, understanding. "I'd give my right leg to go on pirate adventures instead of going to school. Then I'd replace it with a peg leg! Then I'd give my right arm! And replace it with a hook! And then I'd take an eye patch–"

"Wait!" Shivers interrupted. "Why don't you like going to school?"

"The kids at school don't know anything about

adventures. All they want to do is play hop-scotch." Margo scowled. "And I hate hopscotch."

"You seem like you'd be really good at hop-scotch," Shivers said.

"Of course I am! It's the easiest thing ever!" Margo insisted. "Sometimes I try to hop all the way off the playground and out of school. Then my only adventure is going to the principal's office." Margo sighed.

Shivers could see that she didn't want to talk about school anymore. "Margo!" he said. "You haven't finished the grand tour!"

"You're right!" she said, dashing out onto the deck. Today was no day to let the kids at school get her down. She had an adventure to go on.

Shivers grabbed Albee and followed Margo out onto the deck.

Margo smiled proudly and said, "For the grand finale, a grand piano!" She pointed to a shiny black piano next to the edge of the ship. It was very grand indeed.

"My grand finale piano! Did you move it out here so we can have song and dance time outside?" Shivers asked, clapping his hands and jumping up and down.

"No, Shivers," Margo explained. "We need to use the piano as an anchor when we're out to sea."

Shivers stopped jumping. He was disappointed about song and dance time, but he was even more upset about something else Margo had just said.

He had to make sure he had heard her correctly, so he asked, "Wait a second . . . when we're out to what?"

"Out to sea," Margo repeated.

Shivers let out a wheeze, which is somewhere in between a whisper and a sneeze. "What to sea?" he asked.

"Out to sea! Now, enough messing around!" Margo shouted as she checked and double-checked the rope tied to the grand finale piano.

"Hmm. I think there's been a misunderstanding," said Shivers. "I don't 'mess around.' I can't stand messes. They look like monsters taking over the floor! And about that 'out to sea' business . . ."

"Shivers!" Margo's green eyes grew even wider than usual. "How could we possibly save your family without going out to sea?"

"Umm . . . send some really threatening post-cards?" Shivers offered.

"We don't have their address!" Margo shouted.

Shivers groaned. He actually thought that was

a pretty good suggestion for being put on the spot like that. He thought to himself, *I've really backed myself into a corner with this one.* Which was a big problem, because Shivers thought corners were really creepy.

Shivers pressed on. "It's just that Albee's more of a land fish than a water fish."

"He's in water right now!"

"Yeah, but that's *fresh*water. He's got a salt allergy," Shivers argued.

Margo stomped her foot. "Why don't you just leave the stupid fish behind, then??!"

Albee was devastated.

Margo took Albee's bag from Shivers's hands. "I'll drop him off with my dad," she said. "He'll take good care of him until we get back. If Albee is too scared to go on this adventure, we have to leave him behind and go by ourselves."

"I can't leave him!" Shivers whimpered.

"We'll be back by dinner!" Margo said. "Unless we get captured by kidnappers, then it'll be more like a week. . . . Unless we get caught in the Bermuda Triangle, then it'll be more like a month. Unless we get–"

"Stop!" Shivers said. He took a deep breath. "The truth is," he admitted, "Albee isn't afraid of anything. It's me. I'm afraid of everything."

Like a true police officer, Margo was skeptical. She began an investigation.

"You say you're afraid of everything? Nobody's afraid of everything." She put her hands on her hips and stared him down, searching for the truth.

"Well, I am," Shivers said.

"Are you afraid of jack-o'-lanterns?" Margo began circling around Shivers.

"Of course!" Shivers recoiled. "I'm afraid of

anything that involves pumpkins! Have you seen the size of those seeds?"

Margo pressed on. "Are you afraid of pepperoni pizza?"

"You mean deadly spotted cheese bread? Absolutely!" Shivers said.

deadly bread

"Are you afraid of straw-berries?" she asked.

"Of course!" said Shivers. "Where's the straw? Where's the straw?!"

no straw ?!

By now, Margo had Shivers spinning in circles.

"Are you afraid of bubble baths?" she asked.

Shivers sighed. "I once had a dear friend who tried taking a bubble bath. I never saw him again."

help!

"Are you afraid of clouds?" Margo asked.

Shivers threw his hands up in the air and said, "Oh, you mean those cute fluffy pillows in the sky that *generate enough electricity to kill a man*?! Yes. I'm afraid of clouds."

killer clouds

Margo burst out laughing.

But Shivers didn't crack a smile. He didn't even shiver. Margo could see that he was serious. She tried again. "Are you afraid of Albee?"

Shivers raised his eyebrow. "I don't like the way he looks at me sometimes."

"Are you afraid of the ocean?" she asked.

"I wouldn't even look at the ocean on a map!" he replied.

"But you're supposed to be a pirate!" she cried, jumping onto the piano.

"That's what I'm afraid of most," said Shivers softly. "It's my number one fear."

Margo realized that Shivers needed her help. She closed her eyes and thought for a moment . . . then another moment. . . . Shivers wondered if she had fallen asleep. Finally, her eyes popped open.

"Shivers?" Margo asked. "Are you afraid of me?"

"You?" Shivers didn't know what to say. He looked down at his hands and noticed that they weren't sweating. His stomach wasn't turning. Even his bunny slippers weren't shaking. It could only mean one thing. "No," he replied, a little surprised at his own answer.

"What about now?" Margo asked, making a terrifying face.

BLARG!

"No!" Shivers said happily.

Margo climbed down from the piano and grabbed Shivers's hand. "Then you're not afraid of everything," she said. "Now let's go!" She smiled and pulled Shivers toward the steering wheel so they could guide the *Land Lady* to sea.

END OF CHAPTER THREE.

OR MAYBE IT'S JUST THE BEGINNING.

AS THE SHIP SET sail onto the open water, Margo breathed in the salty sea air.

Albee stared out at the vast sky, waving his fins contentedly.

Shivers leaned over the side of the boat and puked.

Margo ran over to him and asked, "Are you okay?"

Shivers groaned, "Sorry. I get seasick."

Margo took a bag of veggies out of her big green backpack. "Here, these might make you feel better," she said. "Try some carrots and celery!"

"Are you crazy?" Shivers yelped. "I can't eat those!"

"Why not?" she asked, worried.

"Margo, I told you! I get *C*-sick! I can't eat anything that starts with *C*. Just looking at those carrots is making me queasy."

Margo sighed. She looked out toward the horizon.

"Which direction are we supposed to head?" she wondered out loud.

Shivers replied, "My mom always says, sail away from the puke."

They agreed that it was good advice, so they headed north into the choppy waves.

It was the perfect time for a picnic. Margo reached into her big green backpack. "A great adventure must have great snacks," she said as she pulled out two paper bags full of food. Unfortunately, she had to eat the carrots, celery, and chips by herself. As Shivers sat on the deck of the ship eating what was left over, he began to think that being a pirate might not be so bad.

Just as he finished scraping all of the cheese out of his grilled cheese sandwich, he spotted

a dark, hulking figure in the distance. "Margo, what's that?!" he asked, his sandwich suddenly tasting like danger.

Margo shimmied up the mast to get a better look. As the black smudge in the distance grew nearer, she could make out its shape. "Pirates!" she shouted as she slid back down the mast like a firefighter down a fire pole. "Maybe the pirates can point us in the right direction!" she hollered.

Shivers was a frozen ice cube of terror. "Pirates?!

Did they see us? Can we hide this ship under the water?" he suggested.

"You mean sink it?" Margo laughed.

"Whatever you want to call it, it's better than facing pirates!" he insisted.

"You ARE a pirate! You face a pirate every day when you look in the mirror!" she said.

"That's why I don't own any mirrors," he pointed out. "Albee, turn this ship around!" he cried. "We're going back."

"No, we're not," Margo said. "Talking to pirates is simple. Let's practice. If you meet a pirate, what's the first thing you say?"

"AGGH!" Shivers screamed.

"Almost," Margo said. "Just add an *R*."

"What do you mean?" Shivers asked. "RAGGH?"

"I mean ARGGH!" she bellowed.

"Arggh?" Shivers whimpered, so softly that even the ship mice couldn't hear him.

"Come on, Shivers!" Margo urged. "Say it like you really mean it!"

Before he had time to really mean it, the *Land Lady* was rocked by a huge wave. The pirate ship–the *dark, hulking* pirate ship–had pulled up right next to Shivers and Margo. It was so close that Shivers could read the name painted on its flag: "The *iPoke*." Shivers had no idea what the name meant and he did not want to find out.

Margo shouted from the edge of the deck, "Avast, mateys, who goes there?!"

A tall, sturdy figure emerged from the captain's quarters, followed by what appeared to be somebody's grandpa. The small old man who looked like somebody's grandpa leaned over the *iPoke*'s railing. "It is I, Aubrey Pimpleton," he replied in a voice so shaky it sounded like the words were wiggling out of his throat. "I am the first mate of this ship and the oldest pirate on the Seven Seas."

Then the tall, sturdy figure stepped out from the shadows. In a deep voice that sounded like pancake syrup dripping down a jagged rock, he bellowed, "And I am Captain Pokes-You-in-the-Eye!"

"AGGH!!" Shivers screamed.

Margo clapped her hand over his mouth, but it was too late.

"Aubrey?" The captain looked to his first mate. "Did he just say 'Aggh'?"

Aubrey Pimpleton squeaked, "Surely not, sir! No one would be so disrespectful as to say 'Aggh' to you, Captain Pokes-You-in-the-Eye!"

"You have no idea what I might do to a coward who uttered 'Aggh' to me," warned the captain.

"Oh, I know!" Aubrey Pimpleton cried, raising his hand wildly. "You'd poke him in the eye!"

The captain frowned. "Curse my name! It really takes away the mystery."

Shivers looked at the pair of pirates. Captain Pokes-You-in-the-Eye appeared to have boulders in his arms and tree trunks in his legs. He only had nine fingers. The tenth, his poking finger, was a pencil sharpened to the finest point. Shivers hoped it was because the captain spent a lot of time writing in his diary, but he knew deep down that was probably not the reason.

Then there was Aubrey Pimpleton, a stooped old man whose head reminded Shivers of a skinless grape. He had one white hair that grew from the top of his head to the tip of his big toe—it was hard to tell if the hair grew from the head down or the toe up.

Margo took a step toward them and said, "He didn't say 'Aggh.'"

"I heard 'Aggh,'" Aubrey said. Then he sneezed and his bones rattled from the force.

Margo elbowed Shivers in his soft jelly ribs. "Tell them what you said, Shivers."

"I said . . ." Shivers took a deep breath. He closed his eyes. Then from the depths of his belly, he bellowed, "ARGGH!" It sounded like he really meant it.

Everyone was still until finally the captain spoke, his sneer turning into a smile. "Why didn't you say so, mateys?! He said, 'Arggh!' What a lovely salutation! Would you like some pie?"

Shivers sighed with relief and wiped the sweat from his forehead. He couldn't believe that these pirates, who seemed so frightening just moments ago, were really so kind and gentle.

"What kind of pie is it?" asked Shivers.

"It's Eye Pie," said the captain.

"Um, no thanks," said Shivers.

Margo piped up in her best Pirate Speak, "Actually, Captain, we be searching for some lost pirates that came by this way, but a wee flea's age ago. We was hoping you could decode our parchment clue."

Shivers leaned over to Margo and whispered, "I didn't understand a word of that."

Margo whispered back, "I asked for their help."

The captain smiled a toothy grin. "Why, never before in all my floating round the Seven Seas has a request passed by my flotsam ears that pleased me so—like salt on a Sunday. I must oblige a wee plunderer such as you standing before my one good eye."

Margo hadn't known Shivers for very long, but she was learning to tell when he was confused. From the look on his face, she knew this was one of those times. She turned to him, smiling, and explained, "He said yes."

Aubrey sent a plump, fluffy pigeon over to the *Land Lady* to retrieve the letter from Shivers's parents. The pigeon fluttered back to the *iPoke* with the letter, then settled in on Aubrey's head for a nap.

"'A Pirate Mission on the Eastern Seas,'" Aubrey read aloud, drooling a little on the paper. "The only mission worth a seal's song on the Eastern Seas is the quest for the Treasure Torch."

"The Treasure Torch!" Shivers said breathlessly. "The one treasure that every pirate wants and no pirate can seem to find."

"Indeed," said the captain.

"Only the bravest pirates even try to go after it," said Shivers.

"Excuse me?" Margo asked. "What is the Treasure Torch?"

"More like Treasure Torture!" Aubrey cackled. "The Treasure Torch is the most famed booty this side of Neptune's nostrils. Many brave pirates have gone looking for it . . . and nary a one of them was ever seen again."

"I'm sorry. But what does 'nary' mean?" asked Shivers.

"Quiet!" whispered Margo. "Do you know where they would have gone to look for it?"

"Alas, I don't," sighed Aubrey. He reached into his pocket and pulled out a rotten chicken bone wrapped in a napkin. "How do you think I got to be the oldest pirate on the Seven Seas? I never went looking for the Treasure Torch," he said, chewing on the chicken bone.

"Can we have our letter back?" Margo asked.

She wasn't going to give up just yet.

Aubrey scowled. "I don't like to wake up Bertha." Nonetheless, he roused the pigeon from her nap so she could fly the letter over.

Margo read the letter from Shivers's parents again and again, her eyeballs moving back and forth like sideways yo-yos. Finally, she pointed to the bottom corner right above the pigeon poop and said, "They wrote down here that we should find the carnival. Is there a carnival anywhere around here?"

"They must have gone mad," said the captain. "The sea's no place for a carnival."

"Captain," said Aubrey. "I might know something about a carnival." He handed the captain his rotten chicken bone.

"Aubrey, how many times do I have to tell you, a chicken bone is not a present! Wait a minute. . . ." The captain looked at the napkin wrapped around the bone. Printed in big, blue letters was one word: CARNIVAL.

Margo asked Aubrey, "Where did you get that chicken bone?"

"Two leagues back that way. Make a right at the giant squid," Aubrey replied.

Margo and Shivers thanked the two men. Albee waved his fins appreciatively. Then they sailed off toward their next hope . . . or toward their doom, depending on how you feel about giant squids.

The captain looked at Aubrey with a glimmer in his eyes . . . well, in his one eye. "Aubrey, never has there been a destiny so clear as ours. We will follow them from a distance. When they find the Treasure Torch, we will snatch it from their unsuspecting hands! Or fins, if the fish gets it first."

Aubrey nodded in agreement, his neck bones creaking. He lifted the anchor out of the water. The *iPoke* lurched forward. And the two pirates began their quest, sharing a piece of Eye Pie as they followed the distant sounds of Margo sharpening a sword and Shivers puking off the side of the boat.

CHAPTER FIVE

MARGO HELD UP THE sword to the sun. The light sparkled brightly on its sharp edge. "I think this one is done!" she called. "When you're done puking, can you get me another sword from the bathtub?"

Shivers turned to Margo, his face pale and a little green. "Something's wrong," he said. "The ship doesn't usually rock this much."

"The ship doesn't usually rock at all, Shivers. It's usually on the beach," Margo reminded him. "Can you please get me another sword? I want to make sure they're all sharp enough."

"How do you know when they're sharp enough?" Shivers asked.

"The ancient pirates always said, 'A sword is never sharp enough until you can hear it cut the air.'"

"How could you hear that? Does the air scream?" Shivers started poking the air around him.

"Let's find out!" Margo sliced the sword through the air and it made a WHOOSH sound. "Good enough for me!" She jabbed the sword in front of her, then spun around and swung it through the air again. She leaped across the deck so fast that Shivers could barely see her.

"How did you learn to do that?" he said, marveling.

"I watch a lot of samurai movies. And my dad makes me take ballet lessons."

"Can you teach me some moves?"

"Sure!" said Margo. "But you should probably start with a practice sword." She picked up a mop and threw it to him.

Shivers caught it in his hand. "But this is what I use to swab the poop deck!"

"Well, now you can use it to conquer your enemies."

She began the lesson with a move called Butter on Toast, where she sliced her sword back and forth like she was spreading butter on a giant piece of toast.

Then she taught Shivers the Party Pooper, where she jabbed her sword in front of her like she was in a room full of balloons that needed to be popped.

"This one is called the Toe Tickler!" Margo announced. She lunged forward, and just as she was about to sweep her sword across the ground, her feet flew out from under her, launching her into a sloppy somersault. She landed flat on her back, her sword sticking straight up toward the sky.

"Wow, that was crazy!" Shivers gave Margo a round of applause. "But it didn't have anything to do with toes."

"That wasn't supposed to happen." Margo got back on her feet and brushed herself off. "Something rocked the ship!"

"I told you it was rocking more than usual!"

Just then, the ship tilted underneath them, and they both tumbled across the deck. Margo jumped to her feet. "I think we hit something!"

"Or something hit us," said Shivers.

"What is it?" Margo called out.

Shivers tiptoed to the front of the boat. He peered down into the water below and gasped.

"I think it's a humongous bowling ball swimming through spaghetti!"

Margo thought for a moment. "The giant squid! We found it!" she said, giving Shivers a high five.

"We need to make a right!" Shivers cried. "That's what Captain Pokes-You-in-the-Eye and Aubrey told us to do!"

He looked up toward Albee, who was sitting next to the steering wheel in his bag. "Albee, turn the ship!"

"Maybe you'd better help him, Shivers," Margo suggested.

"Good idea." Shivers ran up to the captain's deck, grabbed the wheel with both hands, and pulled it all the way to the right. Albee supervised.

The *Land Lady* creaked as it turned in the water. "Carnival, here we come!" shouted Margo. "Here we—oof!" The deck lurched again and she suddenly found herself lying on her back.

"Was that a speed bump?" Shivers called down from the captain's deck.

"I don't think so," said Margo. She looked down over the side of the ship and saw two enormous eyeballs the size of watermelons peering up at her from the water. "It's the giant squid again!"

"Oh! Well, I guess we'd better take another right." Shivers grabbed the steering wheel and spun it to the right. "Good supervising, Albee!"

Before the ship could go any farther, a slimy, brick-red tentacle flopped over the railing next to Margo. She backed away as it coiled around the

side of the ship. "Shivers! I think the squid is try-ing to eat the ship!"

"No! Not my *Land Lady*!" Shivers cried.

"Don't worry. The ship is ready for an attack like this!" Margo assured him.

"You're right! There's that coat closet in my sleeping quarters that locks from the inside. We can hide there until the squid is finished eating!"

"No!" Margo shouted. "Remember what I did with your pillowcases?"

"Oh, right! You turned them into a giant sack!" Shivers was still a little miffed about the satin ones.

"Go get it!" Margo shouted.

Shivers bolted down the captain's deck ladder and into his sleeping quarters, leaving Albee to steer.

Shivers grabbed the pillowcase sack off his bed and started toward the door. But then he noticed how inviting his mattress looked, and how fluffy his blanket looked, and how cozy his Coziest Pillows of the World poster looked. He crawled into bed and tucked himself in.

"Shivers, what are you doing down there?!" Margo cried.

"Just snoozing!" he replied. "I mean . . . uh, using! The bed! To . . ." Shivers was panicking. ". . . nap!"

"Nap?!" Margo shouted. The squid whipped its tentacle across the deck, and Margo leaped over it like a jump rope. She stormed into Shivers's sleeping quarters. "There's a squid the size of a school bus out there trying to eat our ship and you're in here snoozing?!"

She yanked the pillowcase sack away from him and ran out the door.

Shivers looked through the porthole and saw Margo dragging the pillowcase sack onto the deck. He knew he'd never be able to get to sleep without any pillowcases. He took a deep breath and timidly followed Margo onto the deck.

By now, the squid had wrapped all ten of its tentacles around the ship's railing. Its slimy body hung off the side like a meatball covered in jelly.

Margo was trying to open the sack wide enough to trap the squid but she couldn't do it by herself. She noticed Shivers nearby, hopping nervously from one foot to the other. "Shivers, I need your help!"

"No problem!" he replied. "I've got a great idea. We give the ship to the squid and then we all go home and pretend this never happened!"

"Hold this." Margo handed one side of the sack to Shivers.

"Then what?!" Shivers asked.

"Just stand perfectly still and hold on for dear life."

"Oh, okay!" Shivers said. "That's the same thing I do every time my night-light breaks."

Shivers held on to his side of the pillowcase sack, and Margo tightened her grip on the other side. She whipped it up into the air, and it opened like a parachute. She scooped her side down into the water, trapping the squid inside.

"Now, pull!" Margo shouted.

"You didn't say anything about pulling!" Shivers protested. "I'm terrible at pulling!"

Margo had to think quickly. "Just . . . back away quietly!"

"Now *that* I can do!" Shivers agreed.

Shivers and Margo backed away, hoisting up the squid onto the deck with all their strength. The squid held on tight to the railing until Margo reached over and tickled one tentacle, and the squid coiled up inside the sack. Squids are very ticklish.

For a moment, everything was calm. "It must

be asleep," Shivers said. "If it's anything like me, those satin pillowcases took it straight to dreamland." Shivers patted the sack. "So soft," he sighed, yawning. "In fact, I could use a snooze right now." He rested his head on the cool blue satin.

"Be careful!" Margo said, cautiously tying the sack closed. "The squid might shoot out a big cloud of ink!"

"Why?" asked Shivers. "Is he writing a book?"

"No," Margo explained. "Squids shoot out ink to protect themselves when they're angry."

"Angry? Look at this little guy!" Shivers cooed. "He's just like Albee in his bag! And Albee couldn't be a happier fish! Right?"

Shivers leaned onto the softest part of the sack, which happened to be the squid's giant eyeball. Shivers and Margo heard a low gurgling sound like there was a lawn mower inside the squid's belly. Then a cloud shot out of the squid's body like a firework, raining down ink all over them.

Shivers started spitting all over the deck.

"There's ink in my mouth! THERE'S INK IN MY MOUTH!"

Margo grabbed Shivers's slimy shoulder and pointed at the pillowcase sack. "We've got bigger problems than that!" The soft blue sack was now a slimy black mess. The knot Margo had tied was so slippery it opened with one push from the squid's tentacles. The squid squirmed out onto the deck and gobbled up the sack in one bite.

"Wow!" said Shivers. "That squid really is hungry. I wonder what it's going to eat next." He looked up to see the giant squid's giant eyes fixated right on him. Margo began backing up, but Shivers just stood there, confused. "That's funny. It's staring right at me. I wonder if it's trying to ask me what it should eat next." Shivers took a step closer. "We do have lots of leftover carrots and celery. . . ."

"Shivers!" Margo yelled. "We've got to get out of here. Quick, to the galley!"

"The what?" Shivers asked.

"The kitchen!" she said, sprinting off.

"Oh. You're hungry, too?" Shivers asked.

By the time he turned around, Margo had almost reached the galley. He started to follow her, but the squid slithered forward and blocked his path. "Whoa, there!" Shivers shouted, starting to panic. "No need to get so close, Margo is getting your snack right now!"

Margo opened the kitchen porthole and called down to the squid, "Why don't you snack on *these*?!" She held up one of the Venus flytraps. "Shivers, do you remember what I told you on the tour of the ship?"

"I think so," Shivers said, racking his brain. "If you see a bad guy and the sack is already full, throw a Venus flytrap at him?"

"Exactly!" Margo cheered.

She started chucking out flytraps like a major league pitcher. But the squid was swatting the flytraps away like a major league batter—with ten gooey bats. Even when Margo managed to throw one of the flytraps right between the squid's eyes, it flicked the flytrap off like a mosquito.

"These flytraps aren't doing anything!" said Shivers.

Margo glared at him. "Well, they looked a lot scarier in my plant book! Do you have a better idea?"

"How about we make some popcorn? Do squids like popcorn?" Shivers offered.

Suddenly, Margo thought of the solution. "The bathtub full of swords!!!" She bolted off to the bathtub.

"That was going to be my next idea. . . ." Shivers mumbled.

Meanwhile, the squid was closing in on Shivers, with two of its tentacles raised up in the air like it was trying to slow-dance with him.

Margo arrived on the deck brandishing a sword. "Hey, Shivers!" she shouted. "Catch!" She tossed one of the swords to Shivers. He immediately covered his head and ducked. The sword sailed right past him, off the side of the ship, and made a tiny PLINK sound as it hit the water.

"Are you CRAZY?!" Shivers cried. "You never finished my sword training!"

By now, the squid's tentacles were surrounding Shivers like he was an egg in a slimy nest.

"You're right." She frowned. And then she unfrowned. "But you were getting really good with that mop!" She only half meant what she was saying, but this wasn't a time for such fine distinctions. "Remember, Shivers: Butter on Toast!"

With his eyes closed and one hand gripping the mop handle, Shivers swung wildly at the squid like a baby trying to hit a piñata. Startled, the squid started to edge backward.

Margo called out, "Party Pooper!"

By now, Shivers was whimpering and sort of dancing around, still with his eyes closed, trying to remember the moves Margo had taught him. "Oh, just poke him with it, Shivers!" Margo finally shouted.

And so very, very slowly, with one eye peeking open, Shivers jabbed the mop at the squid, and the squid opened its mouth and slurped it up. "My mop!" Shivers cried.

"What will I swab with now?!" The squid started toward Shivers, looking hungrier than ever. At that moment, the ship sailed over a huge wave. Shivers fell and landed in squid goo. The squid tripped and landed in a pool of its own ink. The slippery ink sent the squid sliding right off the edge of the deck and into the sea.

"Nice job, ocean! And, Shivers . . . you were there, too!" Margo said. She ran to the railing to make sure the squid was gone for good. She looked over the side of the ship, only to see that the beast was still hanging on with one tentacle and slowly climbing back up. She whipped around. "Shivers, it's coming back for more! What are we going to do?"

"Um . . ." Shivers thought for a moment. "Song and dance time?"

At first, Shivers couldn't tell if Margo was confused, angry, or just tired of being covered in ink. Then, slowly, a huge grin crept across her face.

"Shivers, you're a genius!"

She bounded over to the ladder. "I hooked the grand piano up to a pulley system so we could drop anchor whenever we needed to!" She scurried up the ladder to the helm.

"No! Don't drop anchor," Shivers protested. "I don't want stay here with this stupid squid! He does not understand boundaries!"

"All I have to do is untie this knot!" she called out from the captain's deck.

"I'm serious, Margo. This is not a good neighborhood!" Shivers still wasn't sure what on earth she was thinking. In a flash, Margo untied the knot. The grand piano plummeted off the side of the

74

ship and landed with a splash
so big that even a pelican flying high overhead got sprayed
with salt water.

Shivers peered
down into the sea
below, but there was no sign of the grand piano
or the giant squid. For a moment, he didn't hear a
sound. Then, from beneath the water, there was
a loud GULP. Shivers gasped and looked up at
Margo. At the same time, they shouted, "It ate
the piano!" Even Albee couldn't believe it.

The squid popped its head out of the water and
started to swim away.

"I guess it's finally full," said Shivers.

"I can't believe it thought that grand piano
tasted good," Margo said, marveling.

Suddenly, they heard a noise coming from the
water. It was that lawn-mower-in-the-stomach
noise the squid had made earlier. "Uh, Margo?"
Shivers said. "Maybe it didn't."

CHAPTER SIX

(The rest of CHAPTER FIVE got covered in giant squid ink.)

SCRUBBING SQUID INK OFF of the entire ship took a lot longer than Shivers expected, especially since the squid had eaten his mop. He was finding it hard to smile.

"What's wrong?" asked Margo.

Shivers sighed. "It's just . . . didn't Captain Pokes-You-in-the-Eye say that the Carnival would be here?"

"Actually, it was that Aubrey Pimpleton who said it." For once, Margo was the one who shivered. "Maybe he was lying to us. That guy gave me the creeps."

"I liked Aubrey. He had a great hairstyle. I did Albee's hair to look just like him!" He held up Albee's bag for Margo to see. "Well, if you loved him so much, then where's this carnival he told us about?" Margo asked. She was getting frustrated.

Suddenly, they heard a soft thud. Shivers looked out the porthole and saw that a chicken bone had landed on the poop deck.

"I just swabbed that!" Shivers moaned. Suddenly, he heard music coming through the walls. There was a pulsing drumbeat, the tinkling of a keyboard, and even the smooth blare of a saxophone. This could only mean one thing.

Shivers grabbed his top hat and cane. "Song and dance time!!!"

Margo had stopped paying attention to the

tap-dancing pirate she was traveling with. She ran onto the deck to investigate the sounds. "Shivers, look!" she cried.

Shivers danced out onto the deck and looked up. They had sailed into the shadow of an enormous cruise ship. Painted on the side in bright blue letters was one word: CARNIVAL.

Shivers opened his eyes way wider than anyone probably ever should. "It's the *Carnival*! It's the *Carnival*!" he shouted, jumping with glee. "I knew that Aubrey was a stand-up guy. You know, I think we really had a connection."

"Focus, Shivers!" Margo took his cane and top hat and hung them back on their hooks. She picked up Albee's bag and noticed that he was speed-swimming in circles.

"Why is Albee swimming so fast?" asked Margo.

Shivers shrugged. "Maybe he smells butter. Albee is crazy about butter. He may look like a guppy, but at heart he's a big fat fish."

"There must be butter on the *Carnival* ship!" Margo said. "And we're going to get to that *Carnival* right now! We've got to find the Fun Hopper!"

"But how?" Shivers asked.

Margo thought for a moment. "Well, the easy part is to pull up our boat next to theirs," she said. "The hard part is to form a complex system of ropes to make a bridge and then to walk over it without getting caught or plunging to our watery death. Let's go!"

"Okay!" said Shivers. "I'll do the easy part, you do the hard part!"

Shivers steered until the side of their ship was almost touching the *Carnival* cruise ship.

Meanwhile, Margo tied all their rope into a bridge with six kinds of knots and a pulley system.

Albee supervised.

Shivers raced back down to the main deck to check out Margo's amazing handiwork. "How did you know how to do that?" he asked.

"My dad taught me," Margo said. "He can tie up six bank robbers with just one shoelace."

"Wow," Shivers said, marveling.

Margo shrugged and threw the rope bridge across the water. It hooked onto the side of the *Carnival* ship. She pulled the ropes tight.

By now, Albee was swimming faster than crazy.

"Albee is really going nuts!" said Shivers. "They must have a lot of butter up there. Maybe their whole boat runs on butter!"

Margo stepped onto the bridge. "If we're going to find out, you're going to have to face your greatest fear."

Shivers shuddered. "A snail?"

"No . . ." Margo said.

"Two snails?!!!" Shivers asked, horrified.

"No . . ." said Margo. "Climbing across a flimsy rope bridge above a choppy ocean full of man-eating sharks!"

Shivers suddenly felt queasy. "That IS worse than two snails!"

"You can do it, Shivers," said Margo. "I'll show you." She shimmied across the bridge and up to the main deck of the *Carnival*. She looked just like a squirrel on a tree branch. A very brave squirrel.

"Come on, Shivers! It's easy!" she called. Then

she scrunched up her nose. "Wow, I can smell the butter from here!"

Shivers started sweating. "Uh . . . maybe Albee should go first, then. He *really* loves butter."

"Okay, fine. But then it's your turn!" Margo warned.

Margo tied a basket to one of the ropes and zipped it across the water on the pulley. Shivers put Albee's bag in the basket and Margo zipped it right back. She gave Albee a celebratory hug. Then she yelled to Shivers, "It's your turn! You can do it!"

Albee waved his fins encouragingly.

Shivers looked down at the icy water. The waves were churning and three massive sharks were circling below, popping their heads up and looking hungry. Shivers called to Margo, "Since when do sharks swim in the ocean? Don't they live at the aquarium? This can't be right. Maybe we'd better call someone. The news-paper. The police."

Shivers paced back and forth on the deck. "Don't worry about me, I'm just going to go lie in my bed and take care of this. I'm going to wrap my blanket around myself and get cozy. I'll see you later, okay?" Shivers paced over to the door, planning to escape to his sleeping quarters.

"That's fine, Shivers!" Margo called out after him. "I'm *sure* your mom and dad are having a great time being held captive!" Margo put her hands on her hips. "They won't mind that you didn't bother to save them! Oh, and your brother, Brock, won't mind, either! Your BRAVE brother Brock!"

Shivers turned around and walked back to the edge of the deck. A single tear dropped from his eye into the ocean, which immediately gave the sharks a taste for Shivers.

He called out to Margo, "I want to save my family. But I can't do it. I can't!"

"You can!" said Margo. "All you have to do is remember one thing: Don't. Look. Down."

"Isn't that three things?" Shivers asked.

"Shivers, pay attention! Keep your eyes on me and don't look down."

"That's all I have to do? Just don't look down?" Shivers asked.

"That's right," said Margo.

"Well, that doesn't sound so hard," he said, shrugging his shoulders.

"You can do it!" she shouted.

"You're right!" he shouted back.

Shivers stepped out onto the rope bridge. He took a tiny step with his right foot. Then he took a slightly less tiny step with his left foot. Soon he was moseying across the rope bridge like he was on a stroll through the park.

"Hey! It's kind of fun up here!" he said. He even bounced up and down a little like an expert tightrope walker.

"See? I told you!" Margo said. "Just don't–"

"I know, I know," Shivers said. "Don't look–"

Shivers looked down.

"AGGGHHHh!!!"

he screamed, frantically waving his hands above his head. In a panic, he tried to run across the bridge, but he slipped and plunged into the water below.

CHAPTER SEVEN

"THIS IS TERRIFYING!!!!!!" Shivers shouted. He paddled his arms, trying to stay afloat in the ice-cold water.

Margo slapped her hand to her forehead. "This would have been a lot *less* terrifying if you hadn't looked down." She leaned over the *Carnival* cruise ship's railing and shouted, "Please tell me you know how to swim!"

"Of course I don't know—" Just then, Shivers felt something swimming around his legs. "Snail!" he shrieked. He looked down and saw that it wasn't a snail. It was a shark.

Shivers screamed and kicked, but the shark took that as an invitation to nibble on his bunny slippers. What the shark didn't know was that Shivers had worn those slippers when he swabbed the poop deck and they tasted disgusting. Shivers breathed a huge sigh of relief as the shark swam away.

He looked around for something to grab on to. Right below Margo, a red-and-white lifesaver was tied to the side of the ship.

Shivers screamed, "Grab the donut!"

Margo shouted back, "What donut?"

"That big, round lifesaver tube that looks like a donut!" Shivers tried to point to it, but a huge wave crashed over him.

Margo reached for the lifesaver and threw it to Shivers. By now, all the shouting about donuts had attracted quite a crowd.

"Excuse me, is this the donut buffet?" a man asked.

Another man pushed past him. "I came for the donuts!" he declared.

A woman shoved him aside, shouting, "Did somebody say 'free donuts'? I heard 'free donuts'!"

Margo turned to the crowd and bellowed, "Forget about the donuts! My best friend is in trouble!!"

When Shivers heard the words "best" and "friend" he forgot for a moment about the sharks circling and smiled. Then he remembered again. And he screamed. They looked more determined than ever, and Shivers was sure at least one of them wouldn't mind the taste of his bunny slippers.

Just then, Margo heard the piercing blast of a trumpet behind her. The crowd turned to see a tiny man in a tiny hat at the other end of the ship. As he walked closer to the crowd, everyone realized he wasn't actually that tiny, he had just looked that way because he was so far away. By the time he got to them, he looked pretty much normal size, except for his very big head.

"Step aside! Cruise Captain coming through!

Cruise Captain, here! What's the problem?" said the Cruise Captain.

Margo ran up to the Cruise Captain and explained, "My friend fell into the water, and he's afraid of . . ." She had so many choices. "Sharks!"

"No problem, little lady, the Cruise Captain has a solution to that!"

He blew his horn again and announced to the crowd, "The first person to pull this boy on board gets a free bingo card, compliments of Carnival Cruises!"

The crowd cheered.

"That's right!" the Cruise Captain continued. "The first person to pull this boy on board, dead or alive!"

Margo shouted, "No! Alive! Only alive!!"

He nodded and blew his horn. "Sorry about that, folks. Correction, alive only!"

The crowd rushed for the rope, which was attached to the lifesaver, which was attached to Shivers, who now was attached to a shark.

"Pull!" yelled the captain. The crowd pulled and pulled. Shivers held on tight, trying to shake off the shark.

"Shivers!" Margo yelled. "How are you going to get that shark off your foot?!"

"It's not on my foot," Shivers called up to her. "It's just on my bunny slipper!"

"Kick off your bunny slipper, then!" Margo said.

"But then I would only be wearing one bunny slipper!" Shivers groaned. "I would look ridiculous!"

Margo sighed. Shivers was so stubborn when it came to fashion.

"Forget the bunny slipper!" Margo insisted.

Shivers kicked the shark and the shark bit back. Then Shivers bit the shark and the shark kicked back. It was weird. Eventually the shark let go and plunged back into the water below. The crowd hoisted Shivers onto the deck of the *Carnival* cruise ship. He was still wearing both of his bunny slippers.

CHAPTER EIGHT

"WELL, CRUISE CAPTAIN, YOU'VE done it again!" said the Cruise Captain, patting himself on the back.

The crowd cheered.

"We saved him!" said one of the passengers.

"We're heroes!" said another.

"I'm still looking for the donut buffet!" said the third.

The Cruise Captain waved a bingo card above his head. "And the bingo card goes to . . ." He blew his horn. "Me, the Cruise Captain! Thank you everybody. Have a great afternoon."

"Wait! Who is he?" an old woman in a pink sweater cried, pointing at Shivers. "Look how he's dressed!"

The Cruise Captain pulled Shivers up to his feet. He narrowed his eyes at Shivers's pirate clothes: his velvet coat, his feathered hat, and especially his pantaloons. "He must be one of the actors in the comedy show!" the Cruise Captain declared.

"Oh, yeah!" a man in bright green sunglasses agreed. "He must have gotten lost and walked straight off the boat! Stupid actors!"

Shivers tried to explain, "No, no, I'm here on a very important mission—"

"To make us laugh?!" asked a woman with a sunburn.

"No, no, it's a life-or-death task—" Shivers said.

"They say laughter is the best medicine!" a man responded, slapping Shivers on the back.

"No, I'm looking for my parents! They've been captured," Shivers said.

"Oh, I get it. It's dark comedy!" said the green sunglasses man.

"Get him onstage!" shouted the pink sweater woman.

The crowd grabbed Shivers and pulled him away. He looked back to Margo and shouted, "We have to find the Fun Hopper!"

"Don't worry!" Margo assured Shivers. She raced after him, carrying Albee, but the crowd was so big and the halls got so narrow that it took a lot of wriggling on Margo's part.

By the time she and Albee were able to work their way through the crowd, Shivers was already standing nervously on a stage. Margo tried to run up onto the stage, too, but the Cruise Captain stopped her. "Sorry, my little puddle jumper, the stage is for professionals only."

Margo tried to think on her feet, but the crowd had stepped on her feet so many times that it was hard for them to think. She decided she would have to look for the Fun Hopper without Shivers.

"Excuse me, sir?" she said, staring at the captain with her big green eyes as bright as headlights. "Do you know where I could find the Fun Hopper?"

"I know where you can find *everything* on this ship!" the captain squeaked. "The captain will show you the way. Keep going down this hall until the noise from the casino becomes almost unbearable. Then you'll see a staircase, and at the top you'll see the Fun Hopper."

"Thanks!" she said, and patted him on the shoulder.

"Certainly, my little rowboat." The captain smiled the whitest smile Margo had ever seen. "The captain will never steer you wrong! Come to think of it, maybe I should be steering the ship." But by then Margo had bolted down the hallway, her backpack bouncing up and down and Albee's bag clenched in her fist, flopping around.

"Ah, forget it," the captain said. He turned to the stage and yelled at Shivers, "Now, make us laugh, funny man!"

Shivers cleared his throat into the microphone in front of him. He had no idea what to say, which the audience had started to suspect because he'd been standing there for about two minutes frozen and sweating at the same time. The problem was, he couldn't think of any jokes to tell. He looked out into the audience. Everyone was staring at him. This was much scarier than the shark.

He mumbled into the microphone, his voice shaking, "Are you guys sure you want me to tell jokes? Can't we just have song and dance time?"

A voice from the crowd called out, "Song and dance time was two hours ago! We've already done it twice today! I don't want to stand up again!"

Another voice shouted, "I got my exercise at the pie-eating contest!"

"Okay," said Shivers. He had to come up with another idea. "Then why don't I tell you a scary story? Once there was a snail . . . who met another snail . . ."

"No! Scary story time is after sunset!" said a man with a gray beard.

"Tell the jokes, man!" agreed a lady wearing a T-shirt that said *I'm with Stupid.*

Shivers leaned into the microphone and said the first thing that came into his head. "Why was six afraid of seven? Because seven ate nine!"

The crowd laughed. A woman called out, "That joke was hilarious!"

Shivers was confused. He thought he was still telling scary stories. But the crowd was having a great time, and Shivers suddenly remembered that he did know a few jokes.

"What do you call a pig who knows karate?" Shivers asked. "Pork Chop!"

Hysterical laughter erupted from the crowd. People were doubled over in the aisles, smacking each other on the back and cheering for Shivers. He was on a roll. He decided to tell his favorite joke. "What's a pirate's favorite letter?" he asked.

Someone in the audience had heard this one before and called out, *"R!"*

Shivers replied, "No, *A*. Because it's the first letter of 'ARRRGHH!!'"

A hush fell over the crowd. No one was laughing. The man with the gray beard stood up. He pointed at Shivers and cried out, "Only a pirate would know that! He's a pirate!!!"

Everyone in the audience jumped out of their seats and ran toward the stage, screaming. Someone grabbed Shivers's arm and yelled, "Pirate! He's a pirate!" Someone else grabbed his ankle and shouted, "Give him back to the shark!"

Shivers managed to slip from their grips and bolted through the stage door. He ran straight down the hall with no idea where he was going, and the angry mob ran right behind him, closing in quickly.

CHAPTER TEN

(Because Seven Ate Nine)

IT WASN'T HARD FOR Margo to find the casino; after the business with the donuts, a lot of the crowd wandered toward the bright lights, and now the place was packed. She had never heard such a loud jumble of sounds in her life: quarters falling, chips clinking, and what seemed like a thousand slot machines all blasting different kinds of sirens like it was the biggest emergency in the world. *Reminder,* she thought to herself, *do NOT bring Shivers in here.*

Margo scooted through the room holding Albee's bag tightly so he wouldn't get lost in the crowd. They weaved through a maze of tables manned by card dealers who looked like they were wearing picnic tablecloths under shiny, silver vests. Just as the noise was becoming unbearable, she spotted a staircase that led to a balcony overlooking the casino. As she climbed to the top she saw three different stands, each with a straw roof held up by bamboo to make it look exotic. The first had a sign on it that said OCEAN COMMOTION! Behind the counter, there was a lazy looking guy in flip-flops who was selling Jet Ski rides. The next stand was called Fly High in the Sky, with a stumpy-looking goateed man at the counter wearing a shirt that read *Hi, I'm the Fly High in the Sky Guy*. Margo guessed it was helicopter rides, but she really didn't want to ask. Then she turned and saw it, and for a moment she was sure everything was going to be okay. THE FUN HOPPER.

"Bingo!" Margo yelled.

"Darn it!" a man sitting nearby in the casino

shouted while he stood up and tore his bingo card in half.

The Fun Hopper was the largest of the three stands. On top of the long counter were piles and piles of colorful pamphlets. The stacks were so tall Margo could hardly reach the top of them. At first she thought that there was no one working at the stand, but then she realized that what she thought was a tall bamboo reed was actually the tallest, most stick-like woman she had ever seen. The woman also had on a very tiny tan safari hat. It matched her tan safari shirt and tan safari shorts and tan safari face. You can see why she would be mistaken for a piece of bamboo. She was munching on a large sandwich.

"Excuse me–" Margo began to ask.

The woman raised a long slender finger and pointed to a little sign on the counter that said BACK IN ONE MINUTE.

"Sorry. I'm just in a hurry and I'm looking for a map of–"

"Ahem," the woman said, pointing to the sign again. She finished her sandwich and then popped a potato chip in her mouth and chewed. Then chewed again. Then chewed one more time. It was one very long minute— and one very chewy chip.

"Okay!" The woman took down the sign and smiled at Margo. "I'm Kathy. How can I help you?"

"I'm looking for a map."

"I have lots of maps," Kathy said. "If you buy a Fun Hopper Pass from me, you can go on any excursion you want. Whale watching, moose watching, watch making . . . And I have maps for all of them."

Margo sighed. She really wished that Shivers's parents' letter had said which map to get. She reached out to grab one of the maps, hoping it might give her a clue. But Kathy swatted her hand away.

"Sorry, kid. The Fun Hopper Pass is for grown-ups only. You should check out our Kids Club. Today, we've got a great game of hopscotch!"

Margo was steamed. Albee was furious. "You don't understand! This fish and I are on a very important mission! And we need to figure out which map—"

Suddenly, Margo felt a low rumble beneath her feet. "What's that?" she asked. "It sounds like a stampede of elephants."

The Fly High in the Sky Guy shrugged. "They must be doing jazzercise on the first floor."

Margo turned back to Kathy, racking her brain

for a strategy to find the right map. "Do you have any excursions that involve dogs and fairies?"

"As a matter of fact, I do."

Margo jumped for joy.

"Ahem." Kathy glared at her. "This is the Fun *Hopper*, not the Fun *Jumper*."

As Kathy started riffling through the maps on her counter, the rumble that had been beneath Margo's feet now sounded like it was coming from right behind her.

"It's around here somewhere," Kathy muttered, still looking for the map.

Just then, a coconut-shaped phone rang on Kathy's desk. She raised a long slender finger at Margo and answered the phone.

"Hello?" Kathy said. "No, I'm not busy. . . ."

Before Margo could protest, the doors to the casino burst open and she heard a loud, familiar scream.

"AGGGHH!!" Shivers was running so fast, it looked like he had been shot out of a cannon. The angry cruise ship passengers squeezed through the door behind him, stumbling over each other trying to catch him.

"Shivers! Up here!" Margo called out.

When he spotted Margo, Shivers felt terrelieved—which is when you're terrified and relieved at the same time. But then he looked at the angry crowd behind him, and went back to being just plain terrified.

"Margo, help!" he shouted.

Margo knew she had to get to Shivers right away. Kathy was still gabbing into her coconut-shaped phone. In one lightning-fast motion, Margo unzipped her green backpack and swept a huge stack of maps inside.

"It's got to be in here somewhere." She hoped.

She zipped her backpack closed just as Shivers reached the top of the stairs. One of the cruise ship passengers grabbed on to his pantaloons, but

Margo yanked him free. "Let's go!" she shouted as they started to sprint away.

"Now's our chance," Shivers panted. "I lost half the crowd downstairs. They're still waiting for the elevator."

Margo tried to hold Albee's bag steady, but he was bouncing all around inside.

"In here!" Margo yelled. She opened a door into a huge dining room. It was filled with tables covered in lace tablecloths and napkins folded to look like swans. Across the room was an enormous buffet with every kind of food Shivers had ever imagined: pineapples, mashed potatoes, peach pie, shrimp piled high on ice, and live lobsters, waiting to be boiled and not very happy about it.

Margo went straight for the lobsters. "We'll use these lobsters to fend them off," she said. She picked one up and tried to hand it to Shivers.

The lobster snapped its claw in Shivers's face. Shivers winced. "Have you lost your mind? That thing is horrifying!"

Margo rolled her eyes. "That's kind of the point."

Shivers assured Margo, "I'll use a different weapon."

The crowd burst into the dining room, and Shivers grabbed a handful of pink boiled shrimp. "*That's* your weapon?" Margo asked him, worried. Shivers nodded and threw the shrimp at the Cruise Captain. The Cruise Captain caught the shrimp in his mouth, chewed them up, and spit the tails back at Shivers.

Meanwhile, Margo used the lobster and its sharp claws to scare off the other passengers. She had set Albee down next to an enormous serving bowl of melted butter and he was getting very hungry.

Albee swam straight toward the serving bowl so fast that his bag rolled like a hamster wheel and knocked into the table, toppling the bowl and spilling butter all over the floor. The Cruise Captain and the passengers slipped on the buttery tidal wave, crashing to the ground.

Margo and Shivers saw that this was their chance to make a quick exit. They picked up Albee and ran out the back door of the dining room and down a twisting flight of stairs. Margo kicked open a heavy door. They ran through it and realized with relief that they had found the main deck.

The sun glared in their eyes as they looked around for their ship.

"Where's the *Land Lady*?!" Shivers shouted.

"It's just on the other side of the deck!" Margo assured him. "Run!"

"Finally, something I'm good at!" Shivers said as he tore off toward his ship.

At that moment, the Cruise Captain burst out onto the deck, followed by the crowd. "There's the pirate!" the Cruise Captain shouted. "The Cruise Captain found the pirate! Long live the Cruise Captain!" He started singing, "For he's a jolly good cruise captain, for he's a jolly good cruise captain. . . ."

But the crowd was too busy chasing Shivers to sing along. Margo and Shivers ran in zigs and zags all over the deck, with Margo doing most of the zigging and Shivers doing most of the zagging.

"What are we going to do?" Shivers wheezed.

"We've got nowhere to go! No way to escape! And no plan!"

"If we had a plan"—Margo panted—"it wouldn't be an adventure!"

She sped off toward the rope bridge that would get them back on the *Land Lady*, but Shivers's zagging was lagging, and he started to fall behind.

Meanwhile, the Cruise Captain shimmied up the mast. He called down to the crowd, "Buffet line formation! Fall in!"

The crowd spread out into a long buffet line, separating Shivers from Margo and blocking his path to the *Land Lady*. Shivers froze. There was nowhere to run. The cruise passengers formed a circle around him, shouting, "Pirate! Pirate!"

"Well, this is it," said Shivers. "My last hope is that the sharks at least brushed their teeth."

The crowd pushed Shivers to the edge of the deck, still yelling, "Pirate! Pirate!" Shivers clambered up onto the railing, but it was too hard to balance. He tripped and fell off the side of the boat. His voice faded as he yelled, "It was a joooooke!" His feet hit the icy water and suddenly, waves were swirling around him like he was in a giant, salty toilet.

Margo had almost reached the *Land Lady* when she heard the splash. "Shivers!" she called. There was no answer. She stopped dead in her tracks, wondering what the right move was and worried that she was going to make the wrong one. If she left the *Land Lady* tied to the *Carnival* cruise, they might never see their ship again. On the other hand, if she didn't go after Shivers right now, she might never see HIM again. She gripped Albee's bag tightly, trying to figure out what to do. A part of her wished her dad were here. Or even Mrs. Beezle. But there was no time for wishing now.

She felt a tap from Albee's bag. She looked down and saw Albee swimming furiously in one direction. He was not swimming toward the *Land Lady*. He was swimming toward Shivers. Margo knew what they had to do. She placed Albee snugly in the pocket of her big green backpack. "We're coming, Shivers!" she yelled, sprinting back across the *Carnival* deck.

She climbed up onto the railing where Shivers had fallen. She took a deep breath and whispered to herself, "Don't look down." Then she jumped into the water after her best friend.

CHAPTER ELEVEN

MARGO HELD ON TIGHTLY to Shivers's arm. He had fainted before the sharks had realized that without some butter and salt, Shivers would not be a tasty snack. They had swum off in search of a supermarket.

Margo reached into her big green backpack and pulled out the maps from the Fun Hopper. They were so soggy from the water that it looked like they had been chewed up by a dog, or a really slobbery baby. She riffled through them, trying to find one that she could read. Finally, she found one that wasn't completely soaked through. The writing at the top was too smudged to read, but Margo was able to make out a picture at the bottom. It showed what looked like a cartoon cruise ship and a dotted line leading north to a small beach. From what Margo could tell, she and Shivers were floating right in the middle of that dotted line. She returned the maps to her backpack and started using her right hand to paddle north, while her left hand held on to Shivers.

As they floated in the choppy waves, Margo saw an unknown shore not too far away. "Land, ho!" she shouted, delighted. She kicked as hard as she could until she finally reached the sand. She dragged Shivers onto the beach and stood over him, worried. His eyes opened and he coughed. He had swallowed too much water and couldn't spit it back up.

Margo remembered something. "A great adventure must have great snacks!" Quickly, she reached in her pocket and found a carrot she had been saving for later, and shoved it into Shivers's mouth.

Shivers's C-sickness kicked in and he puked up all the water onto the sand. It was pretty gross, but still Margo was thrilled.

"Thank goodness! We made it!" Margo said, pulling Shivers up to his feet.

"Made it?" Shivers asked. "What are you talking about? Hand me my pillow. And turn my alarm clock off. I just had the most terrible dream."

Margo couldn't believe her ears. "Shivers, don't you remember when we fell off the ship?"

"You had the exact same dream about falling off the ship?!" Shivers asked. "That's amazing!"

"It wasn't a dream," Margo explained. "You really fell off the ship! Then I jumped in after you, and when I found you, you had fainted. So I grabbed you and dragged you to shore."

"Really?" Shivers couldn't believe his ears. No one was believing anybody's ears today.

"Yes," Margo continued. "It was so exciting. It was like I was a real hero. I swam like crazy and Albee had my back the whole time!"

"He did?!" Shivers squealed with delight.

"Yeah!" Margo said. "Because I kept him in my backpack!"

"Way to go, Albee!" Shivers cheered, and coughed up a handful of sand. "I want to give him a high five!"

Margo turned to take her backpack off her back. But there was nothing there. "Shivers, where's my backpack?"

Shivers and Margo locked eyes. Neither of them could believe what they were about to say.

"WHERE'S ALBEE???!!" they shouted.

Shivers looked up and Margo looked down. Shivers looked left and Margo looked all around. Margo's backpack was nowhere to be found! "It must have slipped off my back when I was swimming!" Margo wailed.

Shivers was so sad that he didn't even want to stand up anymore. He collapsed on the sand and thought about how he would rather sit in a bathtub full of snails than lose Albee.

"We should have stayed home!" he shouted at Margo. "This is what happens when you take a boat out to sea! Now we've lost Albee! He's stuck in your backpack somewhere all alone. We have no idea where we are. We're no closer to finding my family. And now the only friend I've ever had is gone!"

Margo looked away. She didn't want Shivers to see the tears in her big green eyes, which looked so lonely without her big green backpack. "I thought I was your friend," she whispered.

"And YOU lost him!" screamed Shivers.

Margo clenched her fists so she wouldn't start sobbing. Then she remembered who got them into this mess in the first place. She lifted her head up and stared Shivers down. "Hey, buddy," she said with a scowl. "You were the one who told everyone on the boat you were a pirate!"

"It was a JOKE!!!" Shivers cried.

"Oh, really funny!" Margo said. "You know what's a joke? You. Trying to be a pirate!"

Shivers squinted up at her. "That was a low blow, Margo. And I'm not just saying that because it rhymes."

Before they could go on, a food vendor wheeled his cart between them. "Want something to eat?" he asked with a toothless grin. "Maybe a frankfurter?"

"I'm too sad to be hungry," Shivers said. "Plus, I ate about three bags of popcorn for breakfast."

"Well, now I know why it was so hard to pull you ashore!" Margo snapped from the other side of the cart.

"All right, listen!" Shivers pounded his fist on the food cart. "There's no time for fighting! Maybe you pulled me ashore, maybe I pulled you ashore, we'll never *really* know the truth!"

Margo was so mad her head nearly exploded.

"The point is," Shivers continued, "I've got a fish to find. Your backpack must be floating around somewhere. I'm getting back on my ship!" He started walking back toward the sea.

Margo knew that the only way to get out of this mess was to stick together. She ran after Shivers. "The *Land Lady* is still tied to the cruise ship with my rope bridge, remember?"

"My *Land Lady* is gone?!" Shivers collapsed on the ground again and started burying himself in the sand, trying to get away from this horrible day.

"It's okay," Margo said, "We'll just have to swim out to find Albee."

"Swim?!" Shivers shrieked. "*N-O* spells 'No.' We'll have to find someone to take us."

A sailor called out from his boat, "If you need a ride, I can take you on my ferry!"

Shivers thought about it for a moment. "Thank you!" he shouted back. "We don't have any money to pay our fare, but we can sing and dance!"

"Shivers, we'll just swim. Don't be such a weenie," Margo said.

The toothless food vendor's head shot up. "Hey, if you're getting hungry, I've got weenies!"

"We're not hungry!" Shivers said. Then a light-bulb went off in his head. "Weenies . . . you mean, hot dogs?" he asked.

"Delicious hot dogs," the vendor replied.

Margo could hear the gears in Shivers's brain turning. They sounded a little rusty.

Shivers pulled his parents' letter out of his pocket. "Margo, look!" he said, pointing to the paper with so much excitement that he almost poked a hole through it. "My parents said the island was overrun by dogs." He dashed over to the vendor and grabbed a hot dog right out of his hand.

Margo put her own brain gears into motion as she thought about what Shivers was saying. "You really think this is the island with the Treasure Torch?"

"It has to be!" Shivers exclaimed, pointing to the letter again. "They also said there are fairies everywhere!" Shivers saluted the sailor on the ferryboat. The sailor saluted him back.

Margo was still skeptical. "But that's a ferry, not a fairy. They're spelled differently."

Shivers replied, "Well, my parents have always been great pirates, but they were never very good spellers."

Margo thought for a moment. "Okay, so there are hot dogs and ferries everywhere . . . but where's the Green Giant they wrote about?"

The sailor shouted to them, "You want a Green

Giant? Look behind you!"

Shivers and Margo turned around. There it was, the Green Giant herself.

"The Statue of Liberty!!!" Margo shouted, jumping around like she was on a pogo stick.

"Of course!" said the hot-dog vendor. "Why else would they call it Liberty Island?"

Margo jumped over to Shivers, pointing at Lady Liberty. "Shivers, do you *see* what I *see*?"

Shivers puked twice.

"Oh, no," Margo groaned. "Don't tell me—"

"Yep," said Shivers, standing up slowly. "I also get '*see*'-sick."

"Oh, brother," Margo said, smacking her forehead. She pointed up at Lady Liberty again. "Shivers, look what the statue has in her hand!"

Shivers looked up and saw what Margo saw. In the statue's right hand was a glimmering golden torch. "Is that . . . ?" Shivers's jaw dropped so far that his tongue almost hit the ground. He whispered, "The Treasure Torch?"

Margo turned to Shivers and said, "You're the pirate. You tell me."

But Shivers was already sprinting across the island, screaming, "THE TREASURE TORCH! WE FOUND IT!"

"Shivers, wait up!" Margo shouted.

She chased after him until they reached the base of the statue.

"What do we do now?" Margo asked, catching her breath.

"Well," said Shivers, "if we want to find my parents, we should go where they went."

"Where's that?" Margo asked.

Shivers pointed to a sign at the base of the statue.

"My least favorite place," he replied. "Up."

CHAPTER TWELVE

MARGO WAS VERY PROUD of Shivers. They had almost reached the statue's knee and he had not looked down once.

Suddenly, Margo slipped. She caught herself just in time on a hem of the statue's robe. "That was a close one."

"What was a close what?!" asked Shivers, a moment away from panicking.

"Nothing! Nothing." Margo gave Shivers a reassuring pat on the shoulder.

"AGGHH! What's on my shoulder?" Shivers screamed. "Is it a hand?! Somebody lost a hand!"

"Shivers, it's my hand!" Margo said, waving to show him. He sighed with relief. Margo knew this was going to be a long climb. She wanted to make sure it was going to be worth it. She asked Shivers, "You're sure this is the Treasure Torch, right?"

"I know it is," Shivers said. "My parents have told me stories about the Treasure Torch ever since I was a little kid. It's the one treasure that every pirate wants and no pirate can seem to find."

"Really? It's right out in the open here," Margo said. "Maybe you pirates need to get glasses."

Shivers shrugged. Even without glasses, he could see her point.

"Did you ever know anyone who tried to get it?" Margo asked.

"My great-uncle Marvin went after it and we never heard from him again," Shivers said. "But that's okay because he was a grouch."

They had reached the statue's wrist now. Shivers hopped across it and climbed onto the statue's left hand. He realized he was standing on a giant book.

"What's this enormous book?" wondered Shivers. "Maybe it's a clue." He read the giant words on the book's cover out loud. "July IV MDCCLXXVI.'"

Shivers scratched his head. He was thinking, but also his head was itchy. "Wow, whoever told them what to write on this book must have been talking with a mouth full of peanut butter. That stuff is like mouth glue," he said. "Which is why I only eat peanut-butter-and-jelly sandwiches with no peanut butter."

Margo couldn't help but giggle. "Shivers, for someone who's afraid of doing anything, you sure make doing everything a lot of fun."

Shivers beamed. He was pretty sure that was a compliment. Then he had another idea. "I think the book is written in a secret code!"

"It IS a secret code!" Margo said. "And I learned it! It's called Roman numerals. In English, the words say, 'July Fourth, 1776.'"

"Why on earth would it say that?" Shivers asked.

"To celebrate the birthday of the United States," Margo replied.

"You mean, the Statue of Liberty was a birthday present?" Shivers asked.

"That's right!" said Margo.

Shivers was confused. "From who?"

"France!" said Margo. "In 1866, France gave the United States the Statue of Liberty as a present for its one-hundredth birthday."

"Wow," said Shivers. "How do you know that?"

"Well," Margo said, "I guess Mrs. Beezle did teach me one useful thing."

She smiled and ran back across the statue's wrist. She climbed up the statue's shoulder and Shivers followed. They scurried across the statue's neck and under her chin. They grabbed on to her sleeve and swung themselves up to her right elbow.

"This is the most exciting adventure ever!" Margo announced.

"What about the kidnappers you tied up? Or the evildoers whose evil you undid?" Shivers asked.

"Oh, about that . . ." Margo blushed. "I may have . . . made those up."

"Made them up?!"

"Well, I used to get so bored that I had to make up adventures. But now that I've met you, I don't have to do that anymore," she explained.

Shivers decided he wasn't going to panic about this one. As far as he was concerned, Margo was still an expert adventurer.

They were almost at the top now, just a green giant's arm's length away from the Treasure Torch.

Margo was starting to wonder what they would find when they reached the torch. "Shivers?" she asked. "Why do pirates keep going after the Treasure Torch if it's so dangerous?"

"Because it's the best treasure in the world!" Shivers replied, hoisting himself onto the statue's thumb.

"But how do they know it's worth it?" Margo asked, close behind him.

Shivers jumped up and grabbed the base of the torch. "How do they know? Because it's the one thing every pirate wants! Because it's the best thing in the whole world! It's made of solid gold!" Shivers hung from the side of the torch, his legs dangling in the air. "And we've found it!" he shouted, swinging himself onto the top of the Treasure Torch.

But instead of landing on solid gold, his feet started to sink into the torch flame. The torch was not made of gold at all. It was filled with mush that looked like gold from far away, but was more like a swirl of yellow ice cream up close. Shivers could not tell what the mush was, only that it smelled a little spicy.

"Shivers!" Margo shouted.

Shivers was sinking into the gold-colored goo like it was quicksand. "This isn't the Treasure Torch!" he cried. "The Treasure Torch is solid gold! Somebody must have stolen it!"

"Grab my hand!" Margo screamed.

"Okay!" Shivers yelled. He grabbed Margo's hand and pulled her into the muck.

Margo sighed. "I meant so I could pull you out, not so you could pull me in."

"Oh, that would have been a good idea. . . ."
Shivers said as their heads sank under the yellow
sludge, and they were sucked into a pitch-
dark tunnel.

CHAPTER FOURTEEN

(We had to skip CHAPTER THIRTEEN for obvious reasons)

THE PITCH-DARK TUNNEL SPAT Shivers and Margo out into a cold, damp room. They landed on the stone floor with a thud. They were covered in the spicy yellow slime. Margo dragged herself to her feet and turned to Shivers. "Are you okay?" she asked.

Shivers was shivering so much he could hardly speak. "Th-th-that . . . wa-wa-was . . ."

"That was what?" Margo asked, though she had a feeling she knew the answer.

"TERRIFYING!!!" Shivers screamed. "What happened to the real Treasure Torch?! It was supposed to be made of gold!" He shook his arm, trying to get the yellow glop off his sleeve.

"It's all very suspicious," Margo agreed. "What if there is no Treasure Torch?"

But before Shivers could even consider the possibility, the door flew open and two huge guards stared down at them. One guard had a shiny bald head and the other had a single bushy eyebrow that stretched the length of his forehead.

"Congratulations," said the guard with the eyebrow.

Shivers stopped shivering. "Did we win some-thing?"

"Yeah, you won something." The bald guard sneered.

"All right!" Shivers gave Margo a high five. "What did we win?"

"A new job," said the guard with the eyebrow.

"As a pillow tester?" Shivers asked hopefully.

"No," said the bald guard. In the blink of an eye, the guards snapped heavy chains around Shivers's and Margo's ankles.

"As a chain tester?" asked Shivers, still really excited about the prize.

"No," said the bald guard. "You'll see."

The guards dragged Shivers and Margo into a dark hallway. At the other end, a door opened, shooting a beam of light down the hall and revealing a tall, thin man holding a long, sharp sword. Shivers eyed the guards nervously and said, "Um . . . why don't you two go ahead, and Margo and I will catch up."

"KETCHUP?!!!" the man at the end of the hall bellowed. "Who said anything about ketchup?!!"

He stepped forward and Shivers thought he must be some kind of chef. He was wearing a tall white hat and a long starched apron. "*Bonjour!* I am the great Mustardio," he announced. "And this is what I think of ketchup." He threw a tomato up in the air and stabbed it through the middle with his sword.

Shivers screamed. Margo licked a little yellow spot off her sleeve. "I *knew* this stuff looked familiar. It's mustard!"

"Smart girl," said Mustardio. Shivers noticed that the frightening chef had a French accent. He was about to tell him how funny he sounded, but Margo stepped forward first. "Mr. Mustardio?" she asked. "What happened to the Treasure Torch?"

"The Treasure Torch?" Mustardio laughed. "The Treasure Torch has been gone for years. I replaced it with a mustard torch long ago! So that every silly pirate who set out on the Eastern Seas searching for the most famous treasure of all would fall into my mustard trap. It's a perfect little swirl of deceit!"

"You mean," Margo asked, "the real Treasure Torch is . . ."

"Nowhere near here!" snapped Mustardio. "Everyone who falls through the mustard must work in my factory for the rest of their lives! And you two are the latest fools to join!"

"So . . . that's a no on the pillow-tester job, then?" Shivers asked.

Mustardio glared at Shivers. He turned on

his heel, then marched down the hall to the doorway where the light was coming from. The guards pulled Shivers and Margo, forcing them to follow. Just as they stepped through the doorway, Mustardio bellowed, "Welcome to Mustardio's hot-dog factory!"

Shivers and Margo were speechless. The factory was set up in a vast, high-ceilinged room. In the middle, there was a monstrous machine that creaked and wheezed as it spat hot dogs onto a conveyor belt. There were posters on the walls that could only have been hung by Mustardio.

"Where are we?" Shivers asked.

"The left foot of Liberty!" Mustardio shouted, his voice echoing off the walls, which were really just the insides of Lady Liberty's toes. "The only part of the statue that's completely off-limits to tourists."

There were captured workers everywhere. As Shivers took a closer look, he saw that all the workers were . . . "Pirates," he whispered. There were pirates pulling levers to grind meat, pirates using swords to chop relish, and pirates squirting mustard onto every hot dog. Shivers even thought he saw his great-uncle Marvin peeling onions in the back of the factory.

"Yes. Pirates are very good workers," responded Mustardio, grinning wildly.

"Great!" said Shivers. "So, just set me up with a comfy chair, and I'll be the hot-dog tester."

"Wrong again," said Mustardio. He pulled Shivers into the hot-dog assembly line.

"What am I supposed to do?" Shivers asked.

"You're with the relish choppers," Mustardio said. "Take this sword and chop."

"No!" Shivers let out a little scream. "I never finished my sword training. Could I chop relish with a mop?"

"What kind of a pirate are you?" Mustardio asked.

"Well, it's funny you should ask," said Shivers. "It all started the day I was born–"

"I didn't mean that as a real question!" Mustardio shouted. "Fine. You'll be with the sauerkraut scoopers. Take this spoon–"

"Spoon! No way!" said Shivers.

"What's wrong with a spoon?" Mustardio was getting frustrated.

"One wrong move and you could scoop your eye out!" said Shivers.

"Just take the spoon!" Mustardio insisted.

"Get it away from me!" Shivers screamed as Mustardio waved the spoon in his face. "AGGGGHHHH!"

In the next room, over at the pickling station, a woman heard Shivers's scream. She dropped the cucumber she was pickling. A mother always knows her baby's cry, and this woman had the biggest baby of them all. "Shivers?" she whispered.

"Tilda, what did you just say?" asked the tired man in chains beside her. The woman was Shivers's mom, Tilda the Tormentor. The tired man was Shivers's dad, Bob.

Tilda grabbed Bob's arm and said, "He's finally made it! Shivers is here to save us!" Tilda and Bob smiled two big bright grins.

Back at the assembly line, Shivers heard shouting from behind the wall. "Shivers!" said the voices. "We're in here!" Just like parents always recognize their children's cries, kids always recognize their parents' shouts. And pirate parents shout a lot.

Shivers jumped for joy. "My parents!" he cried, turning to Mustardio. "You have my parents!"

Mustardio's mouth broke into a snaggletoothed

smile. "Guards!" he ordered. "Bring them in!"

When the guards brought Shivers's parents in from the pickling station, Shivers noticed they looked different. Their eyes were filled with fear and they both smelled like pickles. And what was worse, there was no sign of Shivers's brave brother, Brock.

"Shivers, you made it!" said his mom. She tried to hug him, but Mustardio stepped in the way.

"So, this is Shivers!" Mustardio laughed. "You said he was the most feared pirate in all the land!"

"They did?" asked Shivers.

"He is!" insisted Tilda the Tormentor.

"You'd better watch your back!" added Bob.

"He can't even hold a spoon," snickered Mustardio.

Shivers's face turned red. "I *can* hold a spoon," he explained. "I just choose not to because I don't want to scoop my eye out! My parents always said, 'Safety first!'"

"No, Shivers," said Bob. "We always said, 'Safety's worst!'" Bob and Tilda threw their hands up in despair.

"So, this is the pirate you've been counting on to save you," said Mustardio. "The pirate who brings along a little girl to keep him safe." He tossed the spoon to Margo, who caught it angrily. "Look, everyone," Mustardio said sarcastically, "the little girl isn't afraid to hold a spoon! Isn't she fierce!" There was an uproar of laughter from all of the guards.

"Little girl?!" Margo rattled her chains. "My name is Margo and I'm the strongest, bravest, toughest–wait a minute!" She narrowed her eyes at the mustard bottles lining the factory shelves. "Shivers, what does it say on that mustard bottle?"

Shivers read one of the labels. "'French's.' Wow, that's funny! You just told me that the Statue of Liberty came from France!"

"Exactly!" Margo cried. "Connect the dots! When France gave us the Statue of Liberty, it must have really been a hot-dog factory so that they could sell French's mustard all over the country!"

Mustardio shouted, "Stop it! Stop connecting the dots!"

Margo continued, "Now the only question is, was there ever a real Treasure Torch?"

Mustardio snapped back, "Of course there was! But in order to sell more mustard I needed more hot dogs. I needed workers to keep up. When pesky pirates started trying to steal the Treasure Torch off the top of the statue, I replaced it with a mustard trap. From that day on, the pirates have worked for *me*!"

"So where is the real Treasure Torch now?" Margo pressed on.

"Don't worry, it's safe!" Mustardio cackled. "And you'll never find it!"

Before Margo could ask any more questions, Mustardio snapped his fingers and an enormous guard marched to his side. "Throw that girl in the Bungeon!" he commanded.

"I'm not afraid of a dungeon!" shouted Margo.

"I said BUNgeon!" cried Mustardio. "We store the buns in there."

The guard grabbed Margo by her shoulders. He was wearing a black hood over his head so that she couldn't see his face. This made him look like the least friendly guard in the world.

"No!" cried Shivers as he watched the guard lead Margo down a flight of stairs toward the Bungeon.

"Enough talking!" shouted Mustardio, clapping his hands. "We've got hot dogs to assemble."

CHAPTER

THE BALD GUARD PULLED Shivers and his parents over to the conveyor belt.

Mustardio declared, "Since you're too afraid to hold a sword or a spoon, your whole family will work the mustard squirting station . . . for the rest of your lives!"

Shivers flinched in fear.

Mustardio snapped his fingers and one of the pirate workers pulled a lever. Shivers heard the sound of old gears grinding and the giant conveyor belt started rolling twice as fast as before.

Shivers saw hundreds of slimy hot dogs fall

from an enormous meat grinder onto the belt. As each hot dog moved through the assembly line, the pirates put it together piece by piece like a big, tasty puzzle.

First, a pirate would hoist a bucket of buns up from the Bungeon. Then another pirate would put the buns on the conveyor belt, and another would place the hot dogs in the buns. As the dogs moved down the conveyor belt, another pirate would top each one with chopped relish. Then the dogs would roll on to the sauerkraut scooping station, and then to the onion station. Finally, the dogs would arrive at the mustard station, where Shivers and his parents would do the job they were to do for the rest of their lives: PLOP. The yellow mustard squirted onto the hot dogs.

"It's perfect!" Mustardio shouted. "They're all perfect!" He picked up one of the hot dogs and did a little dance with it.

While Mustardio celebrated, Shivers managed to whisper to his dad, "Where's Brock?"

"Yesterday Mustardio threw him in the Bungeon," Bob whispered back sadly. "We haven't seen him since."

Shivers was worried about whether or not he would ever see Brock again. But he was also worried about Margo. And he was worried about Albee. Shivers had a lot to worry about.

Just then, there was a loud blast from a giant steam whistle above the meat grinder, and the conveyor belt screeched to a halt. Shivers was so startled that he leaped up in the air, but the chains on his legs pulled him right back down.

"What is that horrible noise?!" Shivers asked. "I've never hated a noise so much in my life!"

"It's the dinner whistle," Tilda explained.

"Oh! In that case, I take back every bad thing I ever said about it," Shivers said. "I'm starving!"

Tilda picked up a plate from beneath the conveyor belt and handed it to Shivers. "The guards will bring us the food. Then we have five minutes to eat," Tilda explained.

"How many hot dogs do we get?" Shivers asked, rubbing his hands together.

"Mustardio doesn't like to waste his hot dogs on us pirates," Bob said. "He gives us French food."

"Fancy!" said Shivers.

"Disgusting," Bob corrected him. "So far, we've had mashed-up goose livers and frogs' legs soaked in slime."

The guards had already begun making the rounds, carrying gigantic buckets full of food and slopping a serving onto each pirate's plate.

"Ew . . ." Shivers said, dreading whatever was in those buckets.

A guard stopped in front of Shivers and his parents. He reached into the bucket with a ladle and sloshed a green, gooey mixture onto their plates.

"What is this?" Shivers asked him.

"Escargots," the guard grunted as he marched away.

"That's not even a real word!" Shivers whined.

Tilda leaned over and whispered in his ear: "You have to get us out of here, Shivers. You're our only hope. You made it this far. I know you can do it!"

"Mom, look around!" said Shivers, forgetting to whisper. "These are the bravest pirates on the Eastern Seas. They all came so close to getting the Treasure Torch. And now they're all trapped. If they can't defeat Mustardio, a scared pirate like me doesn't have a chance." He put his head in his hands.

Tilda looked at Bob with a twinkle in her eye. "Bob? What does *escargots* mean?"

Bob looked back at her and smiled. Quietly, he picked up one of the little green creatures from his plate and, without Shivers noticing, plopped it on his head. "Well, Tilda . . . *escargots* means 'snails.'"

Shivers's face turned as green as the food.

"Shivers!" Tilda shouted. "There's a snail on your head!"

"AGGGGHHH!" Shivers screamed. Without thinking, he aimed the mustard bottle at his head and started squeezing. He squeezed until he had covered himself in mustard and his scrawny legs were slippery enough to slide right out of the chains. Now that his legs were free, he ran screaming all over the hot-dog factory.

He jumped up and grabbed the lever, trying to climb up onto the machine for safety. But he slid right back off, bringing the lever down with him and starting the conveyor belt again.

Mustardio gasped, horrified. "Guards! Get him!" he shouted.

The guards tried to catch up with Shivers, but they were no match for his fear of snails. Shivers had never run so fast in his life. He hopped up onto the conveyor belt and tried to run forward, but the belt was moving in the opposite direction, so he just stayed in the same place. As he ran in place, he stepped on the hot dogs, smashing the buns and dripping mustard everywhere.

Mustardio fell to his knees. "No! My delicious doggies!"

A pirate at the relish chopping station picked up one of the snails on his plate and flung it toward Shivers with his spoon. It hit him right in the ear.

Shivers screamed again and jumped off the conveyor belt. "Drown the snails!" he screamed, grabbing a barrel full of pickle juice and pouring it on his head. Another pirate sent a snail sailing onto Shivers's cheek. With that, Shivers spat pickle juice directly into one of the guard's eyes and sent him stumbling blindly into a pile of peeled onions, where he began to cry. Tilda and Bob's plan was working perfectly.

All the pirates in the factory were cheering, "Go, Shivers!" and "Go, snails!" and rattling their chains. They all began to sling their snails toward Shivers like a fleet of flying boogers. The snails stuck to his forehead and the back of his neck, and some even glommed on to his bunny slippers.

"AGGGHHHH!!!" Shivers screamed so loudly that the sauerkraut jars shattered and spilled all over the conveyor belt. By now, the gears were so clogged with condiments that the machine creaked, sputtered, and broke. The floor was covered in ruined mustard, and Mustardio started to slip around.

At that moment, a final snail sailed toward Shivers. It landed like a mustache just above his upper lip, with one of its long, gooey eyeballs stuffed directly up Shivers's nose. **"AGHH–"** he started to scream. **"AGGH–"** But it wasn't a scream at all. **"AGGH CHOO!"**

It was a sneeze! The force of Shivers's sneeze sent the snail flying across the room toward the bald guard and the one with the eyebrow. Both guards ducked to avoid it, but crashed into each other and conked their heads together. Big goofy grins spread over their faces, and they tumbled to the floor for what appeared to be a very long nap. As they fell, their keys flew out of their hands.

Bob caught the keys and unlocked the chains holding all the pirate prisoners, even Great-Uncle Marvin, who just said, "Took you long enough!" He was still as grouchy as ever.

Freed from their chains, the pirates headed toward a small door that opened out from Lady Liberty's big toe. Being pirates, they easily ran over the messy floor without slipping or sliding— it was no worse than a ship's deck in a rainstorm. They pulled on the door with all their strength until it finally opened, and they ran out onto Liberty Island.

"No!" Mustardio shouted. He tried to run after

them, but he slipped on the mustard and fell to the floor.

Tilda grabbed a relish chopping sword and pointed it at Mustardio. He was trapped.

"Shivers, you did it!" Tilda said. She had never been more proud of her son.

"Yeah!" Shivers cried. "I defeated the snails!"

"No," Tilda said. "You freed all the pirates! You were so brave!"

"Brave?" Shivers was puzzled. "You must be thinking of someone else. I've been nothing but terrified all day. I was terrified when we went out to sea, I was terrified when we met Captain Pokes-You-in-the-Eye, I was terrified when we fought the giant squid, I was terrified when we escaped the cruise ship, and I was terrified when we climbed the Statue of Liberty."

"But you didn't run away from your fears. You ran right through them," said Tilda. "You know, courage is not the absence of fear; it's mastery of fear. We read that on a cereal box once."

"I should eat more cereal," Shivers said.

Bob squeezed Shivers's shoulder. "We all just need a little help sometimes. That's why I put that snail on your head."

"*You* did that?!" Shivers couldn't believe his ears, which were still covered in snail slime.

Bob nodded proudly.

Shivers walked over to Mustardio, who was still trapped on the floor. "The game is up, Mustardio," he said. "Your hot-dog days are about to turn to cold-dog nights."

Mustardio grinned. "You've forgotten one thing, Shivers the Pirate."

Shivers looked at his watch. "You're right! Song and dance time!"

"No!" shouted Mustardio. "You forgot your precious Margo cargo!" He snapped his fingers and the guard with the black hood appeared.

"Throw her in the meat grinder!" Mustardio commanded.

Shivers froze like a Popsicle made of fear.

CHAPTER XVI*

✱ (That's sixteen in secret code)

SHIVERS AND HIS PARENTS watched in horror as the masked guard made his way swiftly down the stairs toward the Bungeon.

They could hear the guard growl, "Come on, Tiny, it's time to meet the meat maker."

Shivers couldn't believe what he heard next.

"You'll have to come and get me!" Margo shouted.

Mustardio let out a high-pitched giggle. "Say good-bye to your friend!"

Shivers glared at Mustardio and said, "You mean *best* friend!"

From below, they heard the jangling of keys, then an old, rusty door creaking open. Shivers looked nervously at his parents, frantically trying to think of a plan. Or, at least, something nice to tell Margo before she turned into a hot dog.

But then they heard something they didn't expect. The clink of metal on metal, then a loud yelping sound, a **THWACK!** a **SLAP!** and a **SCOOP!**

Then, there was silence.

"Ahem." Mustardio cleared his throat. "I said, throw her in the meat grinder!" He pointed his finger straight up in the air.

Suddenly, there was a pitter-patter of feet. Shivers saw Margo appear at the top of the stairs, a big smile on her face, and no chains around her ankles. Behind her, there was a guy as broad as a boat. As he came up the stairs, Shivers heard, "Hello, brother."

"Brock!" Shivers shouted with glee, "You saved Margo!"

"*I* saved *her*?" Brock said, looking puzzled. "I couldn't have ever gotten out of there without the spoon she snuck into the Bungeon."

Margo smiled proudly. So did Shivers.

"See? I told you spoons were dangerous," Shivers said as he ran to Margo and gave her the biggest hug of either of their lives. Then Brock and Shivers did their Secret Brother High Five, which meant Brock gave Shivers a regular high five and Shivers fell over.

Mustardio's face was as red as the ketchup he despised. "You mean to tell me that my trusted guard was defeated with a spoon? A SPOON?!" he shouted.

Brock shrugged and looked at Margo, then said, "Yup."

"He's a man of few words," said Margo. "But he's a great pirate!"

Shivers turned to Mustardio and said, "Your hot-dog days are about to turn to cold-dog nights."

Mustardio frowned. "You just said that to me five minutes ago."

"But this time, it's true!" said Shivers. "Plus, it sounded so cool the first time I said it."

Bob nodded in agreement.

Then Margo marched over to Mustardio. He was still trapped on the cold, sticky floor with Tilda's sword at his belly. "*Now* tell us where the real Treasure Torch is!" Margo said boldly, staring down at his ugly mug.

"I'll never tell!" Mustardio spat back. Tilda

took a step closer so the sword
tickled his belly button.

But just then, they heard a shout from behind
them. "Hold it right there!"

"Hey, that voice sounds so familiar," said Shivers.

He turned and saw two figures standing in the
open doorway at Lady Liberty's big toe.

"Is that an old onion on a toothpick?" Tilda asked.

But it wasn't an old onion on a toothpick. It just
looked that way. It was Aubrey Pimpleton! And

Captain Pokes-You-in-the-Eye was right behind him.

"What are you doing here?" asked Margo.

"We followed you! And we thought we'd lost you until we found this!" said the captain. Aubrey held up Margo's big green backpack. Shivers and Margo gasped.

The captain continued, "And we found something even more interesting inside!"

Aubrey unzipped the front pocket and pulled out a plastic bag filled with water.

Albee was swimming frantic circles inside. "The little guy was swimming so fast inside his bag that all we had to do was follow the floating backpack until we hit the shore," Aubrey said with amazement.

Shivers was thrilled. "Albee!" he shouted. Then he turned to Margo and said, "See? I told you that Aubrey Pimpleton was a great guy. And his hair is just the best–"

"We're not here to give the fish back!" interrupted the captain. "We're here to hold it hostage! Give us the Treasure Torch and no fish gets hurt!"

"The Treasure Torch isn't here. Mustardio replaced it with a mustard swirl!" Margo explained.

"Now give us our fish!" Tilda cried, swinging her sword through the air. Just as she was about to point her sword at the captain, Mustardio jumped up onto his feet and grabbed Albee's bag. Aubrey tried to hold on, but his finger bones were like soda straws and the bag slid right out of his hands.

"Well, well, well," said Mustardio, holding Albee's bag high in the air. "Looks like I'm top dog again. Top hot dog, that is!"

Margo shouted, "Give him back!"

Mustardio grinned at Albee. "You know, all of a sudden, I'm feeling very thirsty."

"No!" Margo cried. But it was too late.

Mustardio opened Albee's plastic bag, drank all the water inside, and slurped up Albee along with it, swallowing him whole.

"What have you done?!" Margo shouted.

Strangely, Shivers did not seem concerned at all.

"Mm," Mustardio said, licking his lips. "I do love the taste of guppy."

"Oh, he's not a guppy," Shivers explained calmly. "He's a blowfish."

Mustardio's eyes widened and he suddenly looked very worried. In fact, very worried was the last thing Mustardio ever looked.

Albee blew up to his full blowfish size, exploding Mustardio like a firecracker. Bob and Tilda gasped. Margo ducked for cover.

The force of the blast sent Captain Pokes-You-in-the-Eye and Aubrey flying through the air. They landed right in Brock's massive arms. He scooped them up and started carrying them away.

"Where are you taking them?" asked Shivers.

"The Bungeon." Brock shrugged. "Where else?"

Just as Brock was about to walk down the stairs, he slipped the big green backpack off of Aubrey's shoulder and tossed it to Margo. Margo put the backpack on, grinning. Even though it was wet and sandy, she had never been happier to have it on her back.

Shivers picked up Albee, who was already returning to his normal size. Then he filled an empty pickle jar with water and put Albee inside.

"Way to go, Albee!" said Margo, patting the pickle jar.

"Yeah, great job!" said Shivers. "Mustardio's hot-dog days have turned into cold-dog–"

"Not again, Shivers!" said Margo.

Brock locked the Bungeon door with a loud CLICK and then headed back up the stairs.

They all took one last look at the hot-dog factory, then cheered and ran through the door onto the sandy shores of Liberty Island.

Down in the Bungeon, Captain Pokes-You-in-the-Eye was trying to pick the lock with his poking finger. Aubrey Pimpleton was making a bed out of hot-dog buns. It had been a long day.

"How are we going to get out of here?" the captain wondered.

"We'll find a way," said Aubrey.

"You bet your one hair we will," the captain growled. "The real Treasure Torch is still out there. And we're going to find it."

Meanwhile, Shivers and his family and friends were looking for a boat to sail back to New Jersey. Shivers noticed Captain Pokes-You-in-the-Eye's boat, the *iPoke*, floating a few yards away.

"Why don't we borrow that one?" Shivers said.

Margo grinned. "I don't think they'll be needing it for a while."

Shivers sailed the *iPoke* into the sunset with the best crew he could imagine. Margo and Albee were at his side. His parents and Brock were on the deck.

His mom called up to him, "Shivers! Try some of this magnificent pie!"

"We found it in the captain's fridge!" added Bob.

Shivers and Margo shouted at the same time, "Don't eat the pie!"

Margo looked at Shivers. "So . . . what are you doing tomorrow?" she asked.

Shivers shrugged. "I guess that depends on what you're doing tomorrow."

Margo grinned, her green eyes sparkling like two big bowls of Jell-O. She watched the Statue of Liberty grow smaller and smaller in the distance. *Now* that *was an adventure,* she thought to herself.

As the ship drifted away from Liberty Island, Shivers grabbed his stomach.

"Uh-oh," he said to Margo. "I'm feeling a little seasick."

Margo turned to him and smiled. "It must be all that *courage.*"

OR IS IT?

AUTHOR BIO

ANNABETH BONDOR-STONE AND **CONNOR WHITE** graduated from Northwestern University in 2009. When he is not writing books, Connor is a director and producer for the Story Pirates, an arts organization that teaches kids creative writing, then turns their stories into a sketch comedy show. Annabeth is also a producer for the Story Pirates, and her plays have been produced in Chicago, Los Angeles, and Louisville. Connor and Annabeth once ran a half marathon together. After that, they decided to never run again.

SHIVERS!

The Pirate Who's Afraid of EVERYTHING

Meet Shivers, the scaredy-est pirate
to ever sail the Seven Seas!

Visit www.harpercollinschildrens.com/shivers for:

☠ Amazing author videos

☠ Creative writing ideas

☠ Storytelling tips and tricks

☠ Writing prompts and activities

HARPER
An Imprint of HarperCollinsPublishers

Art by Anthony Holden